David M. Hartford's Production.   A First National Attractio
LEWIS STONE AND RUTH RENICK IN THE PHOTOPLAY.

The Golden Snare

By JAMES OLIVER CURWOOD

ARose Books
Incline Village

Illustrated with scenes from the photoplay:

DAVID M. HARTFORDS PRODUCTION.
A FIRST NATIONAL ATTRACTION

Table of Contents

Table of Contents

James Oliver Curwood

Born in Owosso, Michigan on June 12, 1878, to James Moran Curwood and Abigail Griffen Curwood, James Oliver Curwood spent the early part of his youth living on his family's farm in Erie County, Ohio. At the age of thirteen his family returned to Owosso where James attended Owosso's Central High School until the tenth grade, at which time he was expelled.

Despite his expulsion, James was shortly thereafter accepted into the University of Michigan in 1898. After studying journalism for two years he left school to live the active life of a reporter for the Detroit News-Tribune. He was paid $8 a week to cover funerals and write obituaries. Soon after receiving a promotion to cover more lively events, James was fired from the paper for falsely identifying a "peeping Tom". But, in 1902 at $18/week, he was hired back to the paper where he continued as a reporter and then editor until 1907. He left the paper to devote all his time to writing stories and novels.

In 1909 Curwood went on his first expedition to the Canadian North West. Enthralled with the wildness of unbridled nature, he then spent the next 18 years of his life exploring the Canadian wilderness and writing his many novels from the inspiration he received. Although his stories have been considered by some to be too melodramatic, his abundant passion and respect for nature as well as the obvious joy for life that exudes from his work has served to endear his exciting, tales to thousands throughout the world. They have, in fact, been so popular as to have been translated and released in many different languages all over the globe and many were made into successful films. They are stories that capture the reader's imagination, catapulting them into a bygone world where heroes still triumph, villains still prowl, nature is king, and love is innocent, true and not without adventure.

Curwood has been recorded as saying "Nature is my religion and my desire, my ambition, and the great goal I wish to achieve, is to take my readers with me into the heart of ths nature." Although he aspired to do so until well into his 100's, a feat he hoped to achieve by exercise and eliminating meat, coffe, tea, and liquor, his life was sadly cut short on August 13, 1927 when he died at his home in Ossowo at the age of 49. Though he may have failed at this one goal, he nonetheless succeeded at what he felt was his ultimate purpose in life - to share with his vast audience his own awe-inspired love of the beauty that is nature and the adventure that is life.

James Oliver Curwood is buried in Oak Hill Cememetery in Owosso, Michigan.

"The Golden Snare" was made into a "photoplay" by

David Hartford Productions, in 1921. Produced and directed by David Hartford; starring Lewis Stone, Wallace Beery, Melbourne MacDowell, Ruth Renick, Wellington Playter, DeWitt Jennings, Francis MacDonald, and little Ester Scott. Curwood was a partner with Hartford in this film. This book contains lithographs of scenes from the film.

Marcella B. Parsons
President/Senior Editor
ARose Books

Deirdre A. Parsons
Assistant Editor

THE GOLDEN SNARE

CHAPTER I

BRAM JOHNSON was an unusual man, even for the northland. He was, above all other things, a creature of environment — and necessity, and of that something else which made of him at times a man with a soul, and at others a brute with the heart of a devil. In this story of Bram, and the girl, and the other man, Bram himself should not be blamed too much. He was pathetic and yet he was terrible. It is doubtful if he really had what is generally regarded as a soul. If he did, it was hidden—hidden to the forests and the wild things that had made him.

Bram's story started long before he was born, at least three generations before. That was before the Johnsons had gone north of Sixty. But they were wandering, and steadily upward. If one puts a canoe in the Lower Athabasca and travels northward to the Great Slave and thence up the Mackenzie to the Arctic he will note a number of remarkable ethnological changes. The racial characteristics of the world he is entering change swiftly. The thin-faced Chippewa with his alert movements and high-bowed canoe turns into the slower moving Cree, with his broader cheeks and his racier birchbark. And even the Cree changes as he lives farther north; each new tribe is a little different from its southernmost neighbor, until at last the Chippewyan takes his place and takes up the story of life where the Cree left off. Nearer the Arctic his canoe becomes a skin kaiak, and writers of human history call him Eskimo.

The Johnsons, once they started, did not stop at any

particular point. There was probably only one Johnson in the beginning of that hundred year story which was to have its finality in Bram. But there were more in time. The Johnson blood mixed itself first with the Chippewa, and then with the Cree—and the Cree-Chippewa Johnson blood, when at last it reached the Eskimo, had in it also a strain of Chippewyan. It is curious how the name itself lived. Johnson! One entered a tepee or a cabin expecting to find there a white man, and was startled when he discovered the truth.

Bram, after nearly a century of this intermixing of bloods, was a throwback—a white man, so far as his skin and his hair and his eyes went. In other physical ways he held to the type of his half-strain Eskimo mother, except in size. He was six feet, and a giant in strength. His face was broad, his cheek-bones high, his lips thick, his nose flat. And he was *white*. That was the shocking thing about it all. Even his hair was a reddish blonde, wild and coarse and ragged like a lion's mane, and his eyes were sometimes of a curious blue, and at others—when he was angered—green like a cat's at night-time.

No man knew Bram for a friend. He was a mystery. He never remained at a post longer than was necessary to exchange his furs for supplies, and it might be months or even years before he returned to that particular post again. He was ceaselessly wandering. More or less the Royal Northwest Mounted Police kept track of him, and in many reports of faraway patrols filed at Headquarters there are the laconic words, "We saw Bram and his wolves traveling northward" or "Bram and his wolves passed us"—always Bram *and his wolves*. For two years the Police lost track of him. That was when Bram was buried in the heart of the Sulphur Country east of the Great Bear. After that the Police kept an even closer watch on him, waiting, and expecting something to happen. And then—the something came. Bram killed a man. He did it so neatly and so easily, breaking him as he might have broken a stick, that he was well off in flight before it was discovered that his victim was dead. The next tragedy followed quickly—a fortnight later, when Corporal Lee and a private from the Fort Churchill barracks closed in on him out on the edge of the Barren. Bram didn't fire a shot. They could hear his great, strange laugh when they were still a quarter of a mile away from him. Bram merely set loose his wolves. By a miracle Corporal Lee lived to drag himself to a halfbreed's cabin, where he died a little later, and the halfbreed brought the story to Fort Churchill.

After this, Bram disappeared from the eyes of the world. What he lived in those four or five years that followed would well be worth his pardon if his experiences could be made to appear between the covers of a book. Bram—*and his wolves!* Think of it. Alone. In all that time without a voice to talk to him. Not once appearing at a post for food. A *loup-garou.* An animal-man. A companion of wolves. By the end of the third year there was not a drop of dog-blood in his pack. It was wolf, all wolf. From whelps he brought the wolves up, until he had twenty in his pack. They were monsters, for the undergrown ones he killed. Perhaps he would have given them freedom in place of death, but these wolf-beasts of Bram's would not accept freedom. In him they recognized instinctively the super-beast, and they were his slaves. And Bram, monstrous and half animal himself, loved them. To him they were brother, sister, wife—all creation. He slept with them, and ate with them, and starved with them when food was scarce. They were comradeship and protection. When Bram wanted meat, and there was meat in the country, he would set his wolf-horde on the trail of a caribou or a moose, and if they drove half a dozen miles ahead of Bram himself there would always be plenty of meat left on the bones when he arrived. Four years of that! The Police would not believe it. They laughed at the occasional rumors that drifted in from the far places; rumors that Bram had been seen, and that his great voice had been heard rising above the howl of his pack on still winter nights, and that halfbreeds and Indians had come upon his trails, here and there—at widely divergent places. It was the French halfbreed superstition of the *chasse-galere* that chiefly made them disbelieve, and the *chasse-galere* is a thing not to be laughed at in the northland. It is composed of creatures who have sold their souls to the devil for the power of navigating the air, and there were those who swore with their hands on the crucifix of the Virgin that they had with their own eyes seen Bram and his wolves pursuing the shadowy forms of great beasts through the skies.

So the Police believed that Bram was dead; and Bram, meanwhile, keeping himself from all human eyes, was becoming more and more each day like the wolves who were his brothers. But the white blood in a man dies hard, and always there flickered in the heart of Bram's huge chest a great yearning. It must at times have been worse than death—that yearning to hear a human voice, to have a human creature to speak to, though never had he loved man or woman. Which brings us at last to the final tremendous climax in Bram's life—to the girl, and the other man.

CHAPTER II

THE other man was Raine—Philip Raine.

To-night he sat in Pierre Breault's cabin, with Pierre at the opposite side of the table between them, and the cabin's sheet iron stove blazing red just beyond. It was a terrible night outside. Pierre, the fox hunter, had built his shack at the end of a long slim forefinger of scrub spruce that reached out into the Barren, and to-night the wind was wailing and moaning over the open spaces in a way that made Raine shiver. Close to the east was Hudson's Bay—so close that a few moments before when Raine had opened the cabin door there came to him the low, never-ceasing thunder of the under-currents fighting their way down through the Roes Welcome from the Arctic Ocean, broken now and then by a growling roar as the giant forces sent a crack, like a great knife, through one of the frozen mountains. Westward from Pierre's cabin there stretched the lifeless Barren, illimitable and void, without rock or brush and overhung at day by a sky that always made Raine think of a terrible picture he had once seen of Dorés "Inferno"—a low, thick sky, like purple and blue granite, always threatening to pitch itself down in terrific avalanches. And at night, when the white foxes yapped, and the wind moaned—

"As I have hope of paradise I swear that I saw him—alive, M'sieu," Pierre was saying again over the table.

Raine, of the Fort Churchill patrol of the Royal Northwest Mounted Police, no longer smiled in disbelief. He knew that Pierre Breault was a brave man, or he would not have perched himself alone out in the heart of the Barren to catch the white foxes; and he was not superstitious, like most of his kind, or the sobbing cries and strife of the everlasting night-winds would have driven him away.

"I swear it!" repeated Pierre.

Something that was almost eagerness was burning now in Philip's face. He leaned over the table, his hands gripping tightly. He was thirty-five; almost slim as Pierre himself, with eyes as steely blue as Pierre's were black. There was a time, away back, when he wore a dress suit as no other man in the big western city where he lived; now the sleeves of his caribou skin coat were frayed and torn, his hands were knotted, in his face were the lines of storm and wind.

"It is impossible," he said. "Bram Johnson is dead!"

"He is alive, M'sieu."

In Pierre's voice there was a strange tremble.

"If I had only *heard*, if I had not *seen*, you might disbelieve, M'sieu," he cried, his eyes glowing with a dark fire. "Yes, I heard the cry of the pack first, and I went to the door, and opened it, and stood there listening and looking out into the night. *Ugh!* they went near. I could hear the hoofs of the caribou. And then I heard a great cry, a voice that rose above the howl of the wolves the voice of ten men, and I knew that Bram Johnson was on the trail of meat. *Mon dieu*—yes—he is alive. And that is not all. No. No. That is not all—"

His fingers were twitching. For the third or fourth time in the last three-quarters of an hour Raine saw him fighting back a strange excitement. His own incredulity was gone. He was beginning to believe Pierre.

"And after that—you saw him?"

"Yes. I would not do again what I did then for all the foxes between the Athabasca and the Bay, M'sieu. It must have been—I don't know what. It dragged me out into the night. I followed. I found the trail of the wolves, and I found the snowshoe tracks of a man. *Oui*. I still followed. I came close to the kill, with the wind in my face, and I could hear the snapping of jaws and the rending of flesh—yes—yes—*and a man's terrible laugh!* If the wind had shifted—if that pack of devils' souls had caught the smell of me—*tonnerre de dieu!*" He shuddered, and the knuckles of his fingers snapped as he clenched and unclenched his hands. "But I stayed there, M'sieu, half buried in a snow dune. They went on after a long time. It was so dark I could not see them. I went to the kill then, and—yes, he had carried away the two hind quarters of the caribou. It was a bull, too, and heavy. I followed-clean across that strip of Barren down to the timber, and it was there that Bram built him-self the fire. I could see him then, and I swear by the Blessed Virgin that it was Bram! Long ago, before he killed the man, he came twice to my cabin—and he had not changed. And around him, in the fire-glow, the wolves huddled. It was then that I came to my reason. I could see him fondling them. I could see their gleaming fangs. Yes, I could *hear* their bodies, and he was talking to them and laughing with them through his great beard—and I turned and fled back to the cabin, running so swiftly that even the wolves would have had trouble in catching me. And that—that—*was not all!*"

Again his fingers were clenching and unclenching as he stared at Raine.

"You believe me, M'sieu?"

Philip nodded.

"It seems impossible. And yet—you could not have been dreaming, Pierre."

Breault drew a deep breath of satisfaction, and half rose to his feet.

"And you will believe me if I tell you the rest?"

"Yes."

Swiftly Pierre went to his bunk and returned with the caribou skin pouch in which he carried his flint and steel and fire material for the trail.

"The next day I went back, M'sieu," he said, seating himself again opposite Philip. "Bram and his wolves were gone. He had slept in a shelter of spruce boughs. And—and—*par les mille cornes du diable* if he had even brushed the snow out! His great moccasin tracks were all about among the tracks of the wolves, and they were big as the spoor of a monster bear. I searched everywhere for something that he might have left, and I found—at last—a rabbit snare."

Pierre Breault's eyes, and not his word—and the curious twisting and interlocking of his long slim fingers about the caribou-skin bag in his hand stirred Philip with the thrill of a tense and mysterious anticipation, and as he waited, uttering no word, Pierres fingers opened the sack, and he said:

"A rabbit snare, M'sieu, which had dropped from his pocket into the snow—"

In another moment he had given it into Philip's hands. The oil lamp was hung straight above them. Its light flooded the table between them, and from Philip's lips, as he stared at the snare, there broke a gasp of amazement. Pierre had expected that cry. He had at first been disbelieved; now his face burned with triumph. It seemed, for a space, as if Philip had ceased breathing. He stared—stared—while the light from above him scintillated on the thing he held. It was a snare. There could be no doubt of that. It was almost a yard in length, with the curious Chippewyan loop at one end and the double-knot at the other.

The amazing thing about it was that it was made of a woman's golden hair.

CHAPTER III

THE process of mental induction occasionally does not pause to reason its way, but leaps to an immediate and startling finality, which by reason of its very suddenness, is for a space like the shock of a sudden blow. After that one gasp of amazement Philip made no sound. He spoke no word to Pierre. In a sudden lull of the wind sweeping over the cabin the ticking of his watch was like the beating of a tiny drum. Then, slowly, his eyes rose from the silken thread in his fingers and met Pierre's. Each knew what the other was thinking. If the hair had been black. If it had been brown. Even had it been of the coarse red of the blond Eskimo of the upper Mackenzie! But it was gold—shimmering gold.

Still without speaking, Philip drew a knife from his pocket and cut the shining thread above the second knot, and worked at the finely wrought weaving of the silken filaments until a tress of hair, crinkled and waving, lay on the table before them. If he had possessed a doubt, it was gone now. He could not remember where he had ever seen just that colored gold in a woman's hair. Probably he had, at one time or another. It was not red gold. It possessed no coppery shades and lights as it rippled there in the lampglow. It was flaxen, and like spun silk—so fine that, as he looked at it, he marveled at the patience that had woven it into a snare. Again he looked at Pierre. The same question was in their eyes.

"It must be that Bram has a woman with him," said Pierre.

"It must be," said Philip. "Or—"

That final word, its voiceless significance, the inflection which Philip gave to it as he gazed at Pierre, stood for the one tremendous question which, for a space, possessed the mind of each. Pierre shrugged his shoulders. He could not answer it. And as he shrugged his shoulders he shivered, and at a sudden blast of the wind against the cabin door he turned quickly, as though he thought the blow might have been struck by a human hand.

"*Diable!*" he cried, recovering himself, his white teeth flashing a smile at Philip. "It has made me nervous—what I saw there in the light of the campfire, M'sieu. Bram, and his wolves, and *that!*"

He nodded at the shimmering strands.

"You have never seen hair the color of this, Pierre?"

"*Non.* In all my life—not once."

"And yet you have seen white women at Fort Churchill, at York Factory, at Lac la Biche, at Cumberland House, and Norway House, and at Fort Albany?"

"*Ah-h-h*, and at many other places, M'sieu. At God's Lake, at Lac Seul, and over on the Mackenzie—and never have I seen hair on a woman like that."

"And Bram has never been out of the northland, never farther south than Fort Chippewyan that we know of," said Philip. "It makes one shiver, eh, Pierre? It makes one think of—*what*? Can't you answer? Isn't it in your mind?"

French and Cree were mixed half and half in Pierre's blood. The pupils of his eyes dilated as he met Philip's steady gaze.

"It makes one think," he replied uneasily, "of the *chasse-galere* and the *loup-garou*, and—and—almost makes one believe. I am not superstitious, M'sieu—*non*—*non*—I am not superstitious," he cried still more uneasily. "But many strange things are told about Bram and his wolves;—that he has sold his soul to the devil, and can travel through the air, and that he can change himself into the form of a wolf at will. There are those who have heard him singing the *Chanson de Voyageur* to the howling of his wolves away up in the sky. I have seen them, and talked with them, and over on the McLeod I saw a whole tribe making incantation because they had seen Bram and his wolves building themselves a coujuror's house in the heart of a thunder-cloud. So—is it strange that he should snare rabbits with a woman's hair?"

"And change black into the color of the sun?" added Philip, falling purposely into the other's humor.

"If the rest is true—"

Pierre did not finish. He caught himself, swallowing hard, as though a lump had risen in his throat, and for a moment or two Philip saw him fighting with himself, struggling with the age-old superstitions which had flared up for an instant like a powder-flash. His jaws tightened, and he threw back his head.

"But those stories are not true, M'sieu," he added in a repressed voice. "That is why I showed you the snare. Bram Johnson is not dead. He is alive. And there is a woman with him, or—"

"Or—"

The same thought was in their eyes again. And again neither gave voice to it. Carefully Philip was gathering the strands of hair, winding them about his forefinger, and placing them afterward in a leather wallet which he took from his pocket. Then, quite casually, he loaded his pipe and lighted it. He went to the door, opened it, and for a few moments stood listening to the screech of the wind over the Barren. Pierre, still seated at the table, watched him attentively. Philip's mind was made up when he closed the door and faced the halfbreed again.

"It is three hundred miles from here to Fort Churchill," he said. "Halfway, at the lower end of Jesuche Lake, MacVeigh and his patrol have made their headquarters. If I go after Bram, Pierre, I must first make certain of getting a message to MacVeigh, and he will see that it gets to Fort Churchill. Can you leave your foxes and poison-baits and your deadfalls long enough for that?"

A moment Pierre hesitated.

Then he said:

"I will take the message."

Until late that night Philip sat up writing his report. he had started out to run down a band of Indian thieves. More important business had crossed his trail, and he explained the whole matter to Superintendent Fitzgerald, commanding "M" Division at Fort Churchill. He told Pierre Breault's story as he had heard it. He gave his reasons for believing it, and that Bram Johnson, three times a murderer, was alive. He asked that another man be sent after the Indians, and explained, as nearly as he could, the direction he would take in his pursuit of Bram.

When the report was finished and sealed he had omitted just one thing.

Not a word had he written about the rabbit snare woven from a woman's hair.

CHAPTER IV

THE next morning the tail of the storm was still bitterly over the edge of the Barren, but Philip set out, with Pierre Breault as his guide, for the place where the halfbreed had seen Bram Johnson and his wolves in camp. Three days had passed since that exciting night, and when they arrived at the spot where Bram had slept the spruce shelter was half buried in a windrow of the hard, shotlike snow that the blizzard had rolled in off the open spaces.

From this point Pierre marked off accurately the direction Bram had taken the morning after the hunt, and Philip drew the point of his compass to the now invisible trail. Almost instantly he drew his conclusion.

"Bram is keeping to the scrub timber along the edge of the Barren," he said to Pierre. "That is where I shall follow. You might add that much to what I have written to MacVeigh. But about the snare, Pierre Breault, say not a word. Do you understand? If he is a *loup-garou* man and weaves golden hairs out of the winds—"

"I will say nothing, M'sieu," shuddered Pierre.

They shook hands, and parted in silence. Philip set his face to the west, and a few moments later, looking back, he could no longer see Pierre. For an hour after that he was oppressed by the feeling that he was voluntarily taking a desperate chance. For reasons which he had arrived at during the night he had left his dogs and sledge with Pierre, and was traveling light. In his forty-pound pack, fitted snugly to his shoulders, were a three pound silk service-tent that was impervious to the fiercest wind, and an equal weight of cooking utensils. The rest of his burden, outside of his rifle, his Colt's revolver and his amunition, was made up of rations, so much of which was scientifically compressed into dehydrated and powder form that he carried on his back, in a matter of thirty pounds, food suficient for a month if he provided his meat on the trail. The chief article in this provision was fifteen pounds of flour; four dozen eggs he carried in one pound of egg powder; twenty-eight pounds of potatoes in four pounds of the dehydrated article; four pounds of onions in a quarter of a pound of the concentration, and so on through the list.

He laughed a little grimly as he thought of this concentrated efficiency in the pack on his shoulders. In a curious sort of way it reminded him of other days, and he wondered what some of his oldtime friends would say if he could, by some magic endowment, assemble them here for a feast on the trail. He wondered especially what Mignon Davenport would say—and do. *P-f-f-f!* He could see the blue-blooded horror in her aristocratic face! That wind from over the Barren would curdle the life in her veins. She would shrivel up and die. He considered himself a fairly good judge in the matter, for once upon a time he thought that he was going to marry her. Strange why he should think of her now, he told himself; but for all that he could not get rid of her for a time. And thinking of her, his mind traveled back into the old days, even as he followed over the hidden trail of Bram. Undoubtedly a great many of his old friends had forgotten him. Five years was a long time, and friendship in the set to which he belonged was not famous for its longevity. Nor love, for that matter. Mignon had convinced him of that. He grimaced, and in the teeth of the wind he chuckled. Fate was a playful old chap. It was a good joke he had played on him—first a bit of pneumonia, then a set of bad lungs afflicted with that "galloping" something-or-other that hollows one's cheeks and takes the blood out of one's veins.

David M. Hartford's Production. A *First National Attraction.*

A SCENE FROM THE PHOTOPLAY "THE GOLDEN SNARE."

It was then that the horror had grown larger and larger each day in Mignon's big baby-blue eyes, until she came out with childish frankness and said that it was terribly embarrassing to have one's friends know that one—was engaged to a consumptive.

Philip laughed as he thought of that. The laugh came so suddenly and so explosively that Bram could have heard it a hundred yards away, even with the wind blowing as it was. A consumptive! Philip doubled up his arm until the hard muscles in it snapped. He drew in a deep lungful of air, and forced it out again with a sound like steam escaping from a valve. The *north* had done that for him; the north with its wonderful forests, its vast skies, its rivers, and its lakes, and its deep snows—the north that makes a man out of the husk of a man if given half a chance. He loved it. And because he loved it, and the adventure of it, he had joined the Police two years ago. Some day he would go back, just for the fun of it; meet his old friends in his old clubs, and shock baby-eyed Mignon to death with his good health.

He dropped these meditations as he thought of the mysterious man he was following. During the course of his two years in the Service he had picked up a great many odds and ends in the history of Bram's life, and in the lives of the Johnsons who had preceded him. He had never told any one how deeply interested he was. He had, at times, made efforts to discuss the quality of Bram's intelligence, but always he had failed to make others see and understand his point of view. By the Indians and halfbreeds of the country in which he had lived, Bram was regarded as a monster of the first order possessed of the conjuring powers of the devil himself. By the police he was earnestly desired as the most dangerous murderer at large in all the north, and the lucky man who captured him, dead or alive, was sure of a sergeantcy. Ambition and hope had run high in many valiant hearts until it was generally conceded that Bram was dead.

Philip was not thinking of the sergeantcy as he kept steadily along the edge of the Barren. His service would shortly be up, and he had other plans for the future. From the moment his fingers had touched the golden strand of hair he had been filled with a new and curious emotion. It possessed him even more strongly to-day than it had last night. He had not given voice to that emotion, or to the thoughts it had roused, even to Pierre. Perhaps he was ridiculous. But he possessed imagination, and along with that a great deal of sympathy for animals—and some human beings. He had, for the time, ceased to be the cool and calculating man-hunter intent on the possession of another's life. He knew that his duty was to get Bram and take him back to headquarters, and he also knew that he would perform his duty when the opportunity came—unless he had guessed correctly the significance of the golden snare.

And had he guessed correctly? There was a tremendous doubt in his mind, and yet he was strangely thrilled. He tried to argue that there were many ways in which Bram might have secured the golden hairs that had gone into the making of his snare; and that the snare itself might long have been carried as a charm against the evils of disease and the devil by the strange creature whose mind and life were undoubtedly directed to a large extent by superstition. In that event it was quite logical that Bram had come into possession of his golden talisman years ago.

In spite of himself, Philip could not believe that this was so. At noon, when he built a small fire to make tea and warm his bannock, he took the golden tress from his wallet and examined it even more closely than last night. It might have come from a woman's head only yesterday, so bright and shimmery was it in the pale light of the midday sun. He was amazed at the length and fineness of it, and the splendid texture of each hair. Possibly there were half a hundred hairs, each of an equal and unbroken length.

He ate his dinner, and went on. Three days of storm had covered utterly every trace of the trail made by Bram and his wolves. He was convinced, however, that Bram would travel in the scrub timber close to the Barren. He had already made up his mind that this Barren—the Great Barren of the unmapped north—was the great snow sea in which Bram had so long found safety from the law. Reaching five hundred miles east and west, and almost from the Sixtieth degree to the Arctic Ocean, its unpeopled and treeless wastes formed a tramping ground for him as safe as the broad Pacific to the pirates of old. He could not repress a shivering exclamation as his mind dwelt on this world of Bram's. It was worse than the edge of the Arctic, where one might at least have the Eskimo for company.

He realized the difficulty of his own quest. His one chance lay in fair weather, and the discovery of an old trail made by Bram and his pack. An old trail would lead to fresher ones. Also he was determined to stick to the edge of the scrub timber, for if the Barren was Bram's retreat he would sooner or later strike a trail—unless Bram had gone straight out into the vast white plain shortly after he had made his camp in the forest near Pierre Breault's cabin. In that event it might be weeks before Bram would return to the scrub timber again.

That night the last of the blizzard that had raged for days exhausted itself. For a week clear weather followed. It was intensely cold, but no snow fell. In that week Philip traveled a hundred and twenty miles westward.

It was on the eighth night, as he sat near his fire in a thick clump of dwarf spruce, that the thing happened which Pierre Breault, with a fatalism born of superstition, knew would come to pass. And it is curious that on this night, and in the very hour of the strange happening, Philip had with infinite care and a great deal of trouble rewoven the fifty hairs back into the form of the golden snare.

CHAPTER V

THE night was so bright that the spruce trees cast vivid shadows on the snow. Overhead there were a billion stars in a sky as clear as an open sea, and the Great Dipper shone like a constellation of tiny suns. The world did not need a moon. At a distance of three hundred yards Philip could have seen a caribou if it had passed. He sat close to his fire, with the heat of it reflected from the blackened face of a huge rock, finishing the snare which had taken him an hour to weave. For a long time he had been conscious of the curious, hissing monotone of the Aurora, the "music of the skies," reaching out through the space of the earth with a purring sound that was at times like the purr of a cat and at others like the faint hum of a bee. Absorbed in his work he did not, for a time, hear the other sound. Not until he had finished, and was placing the golden snare in his wallet, did the one sound individualize and separate itself from the other.

He straightened himself suddenly, and listened. Then he jumped to his feet and ran through fifty feet of low scrub to the edge of the white plain.

It was coming from off there, a great distance away. Perhaps a mile. It might be two. The howling of wolves!

It was not a new or unusual sound to him. He had listened to it many times during the last two years. But never had it thrilled him as it did now, and he felt the blood leap in sudden swiftness through his body as the sound bore straight in his direction. In a flash he remembered all that Pierre Breault had said. Bram and his pack hunted like that. And it was Bram who was coming. He knew it.

He ran back to his tent and in what remained of the heat of the fire he warmed for a few moments the breech of his rifle. Then he smothered the fire by kicking snow over it. Returning to the edge of the plain, he posted himself near the largest spruce he could find, up which it would be possible for him to climb a dozen feet or so if necessity drove him to it. And this necessity bore down upon him like the wind. The pack, whether guided by man or beast, was driving straight at him, and it was less than a quarter of a mile away when Philip drew himself up in the spruce. His breath came quick, and his heart was thumping like a drum for as he climbed up the slender refuge that was scarcely larger in diameter than his arm he remembered the time when he had hung up a thousand pounds of moosemeat on cedars as thick as his leg, and the wolves had come the next night and gnawed them through as if they had been paper. From his unsteady perch ten feet off the ground he stared out into the starlit Barren.

Then came the other sound. It was the swift *chug, chug, chug* of galloping feet—of hoofs breaking through the crust of the snow. A shape loomed up, and Philip knew it was a caribou running for its life. He drew an easier breath as he saw that the animal was fleeing parallel with the projecting finger of scrub in which he had made his camp, and that it would strike the timber a good mile below him. And now, with a still deeper thrill, he noted the silence of the pursuing wolves. It meant but one thing. They were so close on the heels of their prey that they no longer made a sound. Scarcely had the caribou disappeared when Philip saw the first of them—gray, swiftly moving shapes, spread out fan-like as they closed in on two sides for attack, so close that he could hear the patter of their feet and the blood-curdling whines that came from between their gaping jaws. There were at least twenty of them, perhaps thirty, and they were gone with the swiftness of shadows driven by a gale.

From his uncomfortable position Philip lowered himself to the snow again. With its three or four hundred yard lead he figured that the caribou would almost reach the timber a mile away before the end came. Concealed in the shadow of the spruce, he waited. He made no effort to analyze the confidence with which he watched for Bram. When he at last heard the curious *zip-zip-zip* of snowshoes approaching his blood ran no faster than it had in the preceding minutes of his expectation, so sure had he been that the man he was after would soon loom up out of the starlight. In the brief interval after the passing of the wolves he had made up his mind what he would do. Fate had played a trump card into his hand. From the first he had figured that strategy would have much to do in the taking of Bram, who would be practically unassailable when surrounded by the savage horde which, at a word from him, had proved themselves ready to tear his enemies into pieces. Now, with the wolves gorging themselves, his plan was to cut Bram off and make him a prisoner.

From his knees he rose slowly to his feet, still hidden in the shadow of the spruce. His rifle he discarded. In his unmittened hand he held his revolver. With staring eyes he looked for Bram out where the wolves had passed. And then, all at once, came the shock. It was tremendous. The trickery of sound on the Barren had played an unexpected prank with his senses, and while he strained his eyes to pierce the hazy starlight of the plain far out, Bram himself loomed up suddenly along the edge of the bush not twenty paces away.

Philip choked back the cry on his lips, and in that moment Bram stopped short, standing full in the starlight, his great lungs taking in and expelling air with a gasping sound as he listened for his wolves. He was a giant of a man. A monster, Philip thought. It is probable that the elusive glow of the night added to his size as he stood there. About his shoulders fell a mass of unkempt hair that looked like seaweed. His beard was short and thick, and for a flash Philip saw the starlight in his eyes—eyes that were shining like the eyes of a cat. In that same moment he saw the face. It was a terrible, questing face—the face of a creature that was hunting, and yet hunted; of a creature half animal and half man. So long as he lived he knew that he would never forget it; the wild savagery of it, the questing fire that was in the eyes, the loneliness of it there in the night, set apart from all mankind; and with the face he would never forget that other thing that came to him audibly—the throbbing, gasping heartbeat of the man's body.

In this moment Philip knew that the time to act was at hand. His fingers gripped tighter about the butt of his revolver as he stepped forward out of the shadow.

Bram would have seen him then, but in that same instant he had flung back his head and from his throat there went forth a cry such as Philip had never heard from man or beast before. It began deep in Bram's cavernous chest, like the rolling of a great drum, and ended in a wailing shriek that must have carried for miles over the open plain—the call of the master to his pack, of the man-beast to his brothers. It may be that even before the cry was finished some super-instinct had warned Bram Johnson of a danger which he had not seen. The cry was cut short. It ended in a hissing gasp, as steam is cut off by a valve. Before Philip's startled senses had adjusted themselves to action Bram was off, and as his huge strides carried him swiftly through the starlight the cry that had been on his lips was replaced by the strange, mad laugh that Pierre Breault had described with a shiver of fear. Without moving, Philip called after him:

"Bram—Bram Johnson—stop!   In the name of the King—"

It was the old formula, the words that carried with them the majesty and power of Law throughout the northland. Bram heard them. But he did not stop. He sped on more swiftly, and again Philip called his name.

"Bram—Bram Johnson—"

The laugh came back again. It was weird and chuckling, as though Bram was laughing at him.

In the starlight Philip flung up his revolver. He did not aim to hit. Twice he fired over Bram's head and shoulders, so close that the fugitive must have heard the whine of the bullets.

"Bram—Bram Johnson!" he shouted a third time.

His pistol arm relaxed and dropped to his side, and he stood staring after the great figure that was now no more than a shadow in the gloom. And then it was swallowed up entirely. Once more he was alone under the stars, encompassed by a world of nothingness. He felt, all at once, that he had been a very great fool. He had played his part like a child; even his voice had trembled as he called out Bram's name. And Bram—even Bram—had laughed at him.

Very soon he would pay the price of his stupidity—of his slowness to act. It was thought of that which quickened his pulse as he stared out into the white space into which Bram had gone. Before the night was over Bram would return, and with him would come the wolves.

With a shudder Philip thought of Corporal Lee as he turned back through the scrub to the big rock where he had made his camp.

The picture that flashed into his mind of the fate of the two men from Churchill added to the painful realization of his own immediate peril—a danger brought upon himself by an almost inconceivable stupidity. Philip was no more than the average human with good red blood in his veins. A certain amount of personal hazard held a fascination for him, but he had also the very great human desire to hold a fairly decent hand in any game of chance he entered. It was the oppressive conviction that he had no chance now that stunned him. For a few minutes he stood over the spot where his fire had been, a film of steam rising into his face, trying to adjust his mind to some sort of logical action. He was not afraid of Bram. He would quite cheerfully have gone out and fought open-handedly for his man, even though he had seen that Bram was a giant. This much he told himself, as he fingered the breech of his rifle, and listened.

But it was not Bram who would fight. The wolves would come. He probably would not see Bram again. He would hear only his laugh, or his great voice urging on his pack, as Corporal Lee and the other man had heard it.

That Bram would not return for vengeance never for a moment entered his analysis of the situation. By firng after his man Philip had too clearly disclosed his identity and his business; and Bram, fighting for his own existence, would be a fool not to rid himself of an immediate and dangerous enemy.

And then, for the first time since he had returned from the edge of the Barren, Philip saw the man again as he had seen him standing under the white glow of the stars. And it struck him, all at once, that Bram had been unarmed. Comprehension of this fact, slow as it had been, worked a swift and sudden hope in him, and his eyes took in quickly the larger trees about him. From a tree he could fight the pack and kill them one by one. He had a rifle and a revolver, and plenty of ammunition. The advantage would lay all with him. But if he was treed, and Bram happened to have a rifle—

He put on the heavy coat he had thrown off near the fire, filled his pockets with loose ammunition, and hunted for the tree he wanted. He found it a hundred yards from his camp. It was a gnarled and wind-blown spruce six inches in diameter, standing in an open. In this open Philip knew that he could play havoc with the pack. On the other hand, if Bram possessed a rifle, the gamble was against him. Perched in the tree, silhouetted against the stars that made the night like day, he would be an easy victim. Bram could pick him off without showing himself. But it was his one chance, and he took it.

CHAPTER VI

An hour later Philip looked at his watch. It was close to midnight. In that hour his nerves had been keyed to a tension that was almost at the breaking point. Not a sound came from off the Barren or from out of the scrub timber that did not hold a mental and physical shock for him. He believed that Bram and his pack would come up quietly; that he would not hear the man's footsteps or the soft pads of his beasts until they were very near. Twice a great snow owl fluttered over his head. A third time it pounced down upon a white hare back in the shrub, and for an instant Philip thought the time had come. The little white foxes, curious as children, startled him most. Half a dozen times they sent through him the sharp thrill of anticipation, and twice they made him climb his tree.

After that hour the reaction came, and with the steadying of his nerves and the quieter pulse of his blood Philip began to ask himself if he was going to escape the ordeal which a short time before he had accepted as a certainty. Was it possible that his shots had frightened Bram? He could not believe that. Cowardice was the last thing he would associate with the strange man he had seen in the starlight. Vividly he saw Bram's face again. And now, after the almost unbearable strain he had been under, a mysterious *something* that had been in that face impinged itself upon him above all other things. Wild and savage as the face had been, he had seen in it the unutterable pathos of a creature without hope. In that moment, even as caution held him listening for the approach of danger, he no longer felt the quickening thrill of man on the hunt for man. He could not have explained the change in himself—the swift reaction of thought and emotion that filled him with a mastering sympathy for Bram Johnson.

He waited, and less and less grew his fear of the wolves. Even more clearly he saw Bram as the time passed; the hunted look in the man's eyes, even as he hunted—the loneliness of him as he had stood listening for a sound from the only friends he had—the padded beasts ahead. In spite of Bram's shrieking cry to his pack, and the strangeness of the laugh that had floated back out of the white night after the shots, Philip was convinced that he was not mad. He had heard of men whom loneliness had killed. He had known one—Pelletier, up at Point Fullerton, on the Arctic. He could repeat by heart the diary Pelletier had left scribbled on his cabin door. It was worse than madness. To Pelletier death had come at last as a friend. And Bram had been like that—dead to human comradeship for years. And yet—

Under it all, in Philip's mind, ran the thought of the woman's hair. In Pierre Breault's cabin he had not given voice to the suspicion that had flashed upon him. He had kept it to himself, and Pierre, afraid to speak because of the horror of it, had remained as silent as he. The thought oppressed him now. He knew that human hair retained its life and its gloss indefinitely, and that Bram might have had the golden snare for years. It was quite reasonable to suppose that he had bartered for it with some white man in the years before he had become an outlaw, and that some curious fancy or superstition had inspired him in its possession. But Philip had ceased to be influenced by reason alone. Sharply opposed to reason was that consciousness within him which told him that the hair had been freshly cut from a woman's head. He had no argument with which to drive home the logic of this belief even with himself, and yet he found it impossible not to accept that belief fully and unequivocally. There was, or *had* been, a woman with Bram—and as he thought of the length and beauty and rare texture of the silken strand in his pocket he could not repress a shudder at the possibilities the situation involved. Bram—and a woman! And a woman with hair like that!

He left his tree after a time. For another hour he paced slowly back and forth at the edge of the Barren, his senses still keyed to the highest point of caution. Then he rebuilt his fire, pausing every few moments in the operation to listen for a suspicious sound. It was very cold. He noticed, after a little, that the weird sound of the lights over the Pole had become only a ghostly whisper. The stars were growing dimmer, and he watched them as they seemed slowly to recede farther and farther away from the world of which he was a part. This dying out of the stars always interested him. It was one of the miracles of the northern world that lay just under the long Arctic night which, a few hundred miles beyond the Barren, was now at its meridian. It seemed to him as though ten thousand invisible hands were sweeping under the heavens extinguishing the lights first in ones and twos and then in whole constellations. It preceded by perhaps half an hour the utter and chaotic blackness that comes before the northern dawn, and it was this darkness that Philip dreaded as he waited beside his fire.

In the impenetrable gloom of that hour Bram might come. It was, possible that he had been waiting for that darkness. Philip looked at his watch. It was four o'clock. Once more he went to his tree, and waited. In another quarter of an hour he could not see the tree beside which he stood. And Bram did not come. With the beginning of the gray dawn Philip rebuilt his fire for the third time and prepared to cook his breakfast. He felt the need of coffee—strong coffee—and he boiled himself a double ration. At seven o'clock he was ready to take up the trail.

He believed now that some mysterious and potent force had restrained Bram Johnson from taking advantage of the splendid opportunity of that night to rid himself of an enemy. As he made his way through the scrub timber along the edge of the Barren it was with the feeling that he no longer desired Bram as a prisoner. A thing more interesting than Bram had entered into the adventure. It was the golden snare. Not with Bram himself, but only at the end of Bram's trail would he find what the golden snare stood for. There he would discover the mystery and the tragedy of it, if it meant anything at all. He appreciated the extreme hazard of following Bram to his long hidden retreat. The man he might outwit in pursuit and overcome in fair fight, if it came to a fight, but against the pack he was fighting tremendous odds.

What these odds meant had not fully gripped him until he came cautiously out of the timber half an hour later and saw what was left of the caribou the pack had killed. The bull had fallen within fifty yards of the edge of the scrub. For a radius of twenty feet about it the snow was beaten hard by the footprints of beasts, and this arena was stained red with blood and scattered thickly with bits of flesh, broken bones and patches of hide. Philip could see where Bram had come in on the run, and where he had kicked off his snowshoes. After that his great moccasin tracks mingled with those of the wolves. Bram had evidently come in time to save the hind quarters, which had been dragged to a spot well out of the red ring of slaughter. After that the stars must have looked down upon an amazing scene. The hungry horde had left scarcely more than the disemboweled offal. Where Bram had dragged his meat there was a real circle worn by moccasin tracks, and here, too, were small bits of flesh scattered about—the discarded remnants of Bram's own feast.

The snow told as clearly as a printed page what had happened after that. Its story amazed Philip. From somewhere Bram had produced a sledge, and on this sledge he had loaded what remained of the caribou meat. From the marks in the snow Philip saw that it had been of the low *ootapanask* type, but that it was longer and broader than any sledge he had ever seen. He did not have to guess at what had happened. Everything was too clear for that. Far back on the Barren Bram had loosed his pack at sight of the caribou, and the pursuit and kill had followed. After that, when beasts and man had gorged themselves, they had returned through the night for the sledge. Bram had made a wide detour so that he would not again pass near the finger of scrub timber that concealed his enemy, and with a curious quickening of the blood in his veins Philip observed how closely the pack hung at his heels. The man was master—absolutely. Later they had returned with the sledge, Bram had loaded his meat, and with his pack had struck out straight north over the Barren. Every wolf was in harness and Bram rode on the sledge.

Philip drew a deep breath. He was learning new things about Bram Johnson. First he assured himself that Bram was not afraid, and that his disappearance could not be called a flight. If fear of capture had possessed him he would not have returned for his meat. Suddenly he recalled Pierre Breault's story of how Bram had carried off the haunches of a bull upon his shoulders as easily as a child might have carried a toy gun, and he wondered why Bram—instead of returning for the meat this night—had not carried the meat to his sledge. It would have saved time and distance. He was beginning to give Bram credit for a deeply mysterious strategy. There was some definite reason why he had not made an attack with his wolves that night. There was a reason for the wide detour around the point of timber, and there was a still more inexplicable reason why he had come back with his sledge for the meat, instead of carrying his meat to the sledge. The caribou haunch had not weighed more than sixty or seventy pounds, which was scarcely half a burden for Bram's powerful shoulders.

In the edge of the timber, where he could secure wood for his fire, Philip began to prepare. He cooked food for six days. Three days he would follow Bram out into that unmapped and treeless space—the Great Barren. Beyond that it would be impossible to go without dogs or sledge. Three days out, and three days back—and even at that he would be playing a thrilling game with death. In the heart of the Barren a menace greater than Bram and his wolves would be impending. It was storm.

His heart sank a little as he set out straight north, marking the direction by the point of his compass. It was a gray and sunless day. Beyond him for a distance the Barren was a white plain, and this plain seemed always to be merging not very far ahead into the purple haze of the sky. At the end of an hour he was in the center of a vast amphitheater which was filled with the gloom and the stillness of death. Behind him the thin fringe of the forest had disappeared. The rim of the sky was like a leaden thing, widening only as he advanced. Under that sky, and imprisoned within its circular walls, he knew that men had gone mad; he felt already the crushing oppression of an appalling loneliness, and for another hour he fought an almost irresistible desire to turn back. Not a rock or a shrub rose to break the monotony, and over his head—so low that at times it seemed as though he might have flung a stone up to them—dark clouds rolled sullenly from out of the north and east.

Half a dozen times in those first two hours he looked at his compass. Not once in that time did Bram diverge from his steady course into the north. In the gray gloom, without a stone or a tree to mark his way, his sense of orientation was directing him as infallibly as the sensitive needle of the instrument which Philip carried.

It was in the third hour, seven or eight miles from the scene of slaughter, that Philip came upon the first stopping place of the sledge. The wolves had not broken their traveling rank, and for this reason he guessed that Bram had paused only long enough to put on his snowshoes. After this Philip could measure quite accurately the speed of the outlaw and his pack. Bram's snowshoe strides were from twelve to sixteen inches longer than his own, and there was little doubt that Bram was traveling six miles to his four.

It was one o'clock when Philip stopped to eat his dinner. He figured that he was fifteen miles from the timber-line. As he ate there pressed upon him more and more persistently the feeling that he had entered upon an adventure which was leading toward inevitable disaster for him. For the first time the significance of Bram's supply of meat secured by the outlaw at the last moment before starting out into the Barren, appeared to him with a clearness that filled him with uneasiness. It meant that Bram required three or four days' rations for himself and his pack in crossing this sea of desolation that reached in places to the Artic. In that time, if necessity was driving him, he could cover a hundred and fifty miles, while Philip could make less than a hundred.

Until three o'clock in the afternoon he followed steadily over Bram's trail. He would have pursued for another hour if a huge and dome-shaped snowdrift had not risen in his path. In the big drift he decided to make his house for the night. It was an easy matter—a trick learned of the Eskimo. With his belt-ax he broke through the thick crust of the drift, using care that the "door" he thus opened into it was only large enough for the entrance of his body. Using a snowshoe as a shovel he then began digging out the soft interior of the drift, burrowing a two foot tunnel until he was well back from the door, where he made himself a chamber large enough for his sleeping-bag. The task employed him less than an hour, and when his bed was made, and he stood in front of the door to his igloo, his spirits began to return. The assurance that he had a home at his back in which neither cold nor storm could reach him inspired him with an optimism which he had not felt at any time during the day.

From the timber he had borne a precious bundle of finely split kindlings of pitch-filled spruce, and with a handful of these he built himself a tiny fire over which, on a longer stick brought for the purpose, he suspended his tea pail, packed with snow. The crackling of the flames set him whistling. Darkness was falling swiftly about him. By the time his tea was ready and he had warmed his cold bannock and bacon the gloom was like a black curtain that he might have slit with a knife. Not a star was visible in the sky. Twenty feet on either side of him he could not see the surface of the snow. Now and then he added a bit of his kindling to the dying embers, and in the glow of the last stick he smoked his pipe, and as he smoked he drew from his wallet the golden snare. Coiled in the hollow of his hand and catching the red light of the pitch-laden fagot it shone with the rich luster of rare metal. Not until the pitch was burning itself out in a final sputter of flame did Philip replace it in the wallet.

With the going of the fire an utter and chaotic blackness shut him in. Feeling his way he crawled through the door of his tunnel, over the inside of which he had fastened as a flap his silk service tent. Then he stretched himself out in his sleeping-bag. It was surprisingly comfortable. Since he had left Breault's cabin he had not enjoyed such a bed. And last night he had not slept at all. He fell into deep sleep. The hours and the night passed over him. He did not hear the wailing of the wind that came with the dawn. When day followed dawn there were other sounds which he did not hear. His inner consciousness, the guardian of his sleep, cried for him to arouse himself. It pounded like a little hand in his brain, and at last he began to move restlessly, and twist in his sleeping-bag. His eyes shot open suddenly. The light of day filled his tunnel. He looked toward the "door" which he had covered with his tent.

The tent was gone.

In its place was framed a huge shaggy head, and Philip found himself staring straight into the eyes of Bram Johnson.

CHAPTER VII

PHILIP was not unaccustomed to the occasional mental and physical shock which is an inevitable accompaniment of the business of Law in the northland. But never had he felt quite the same stir in his blood as now—when he found himself looking down the short tunnel into the face of the man he was hunting.

There come now and then moments in which a curious understanding is impinged upon one without loss of time in reason and surmise—and this was one of those moments for Philip. His first thought as he saw the great wild face in the door of his tunnel was that Bram had been looking at him for some time—while he was asleep; and that if the desire to kill had been in the outlaw's breast he might have achieved his purpose with very little trouble. Equally swift was his observance of the fact that the tent with which he had covered the aperture was gone, and that his rifle, with the weight of which he had held the tent in place, had disappeared. Bram had secured possession of them before he had roused himself.

It was not the loss of these things, or entirely Bram's sudden and unexpected appearance, that sent through him the odd thrill.which he experienced. It was Bram's face, his eyes, the tense and mysterious earnestness that was in his gaze. It was not the watchfulness of a victor looking at his victim. In it there was no sign of hatred or of exultation. There was not even unfriendliness there. Rather it was the study of one filled with doubt and uneasiness, and confronted by a question—which he could not answer. There was not a line of the face which Philip could not see now—its high cheek-bones, its wide cheeks, the low forehead, the flat nose, the thick lips. Only the eyes kept it from being a terrible face. Straight down through the generations Bram must have inherited those eyes from some woman of the past. They were strange things in that wild and hunted creature's face— gray eyes, large, beautiful. With the face taken away they would have been wonderful.

For a full minute not a sound passed between the two men. Philip's hand had slipped to the butt of his revolver, but he had no intention of using it. Then he found his voice. It seemed the most natural thing in the world that he should say what he did.

"Hello, Bram!"

"*Boo-joo*, m'sieu!"

Only Bram's thick lips moved. His voice was low and guttural. Almost instantly his head disappeared from the opening.

Philip dug himself quickly from his sleeping-bag. Through the aperture there came to him now another sound, the yearning whine of beasts. He could not hear Bram.

In spite of the confidence which his first look at Bram had given him he felt a sudden shiver run up his spine as he faced the end of the tunnel on his hands and knees, his revolver in his hand. What a rat in a trap he would be if Bram loosed his wolves! What sport for the pack—and perhaps for the master himself! He could kill two or three—and that would be all. They would be in on him like a whirlwind, diving through his snow walls as easily as a swimmer might cut through water. Had he twice made a fool of himself? Should he have winged Bram Johnson, three times a murderer, in place of offering him a greeting?

He began crawling toward the opening, and again he heard the snarl and whine of the beasts. The sound seemed some distance away. He reached the end of the tunnel and peered out through the "door" he had made in the crust.

From his position he could see nothing—nothing but the endless sweep of the Barren and his old trail leading up to the snow dune. The muzzle of his revolver was at the aperture when he heard Bram's voice.

"M'sieu—ze revolv'— ze knife or I mus' keel you. Ze wolve plent' hungr'—"

Bram was standing just outside of his line of vision. He had not spoken loudly or threateningly, but Philip felt in the words a cold and unexcited deadliness of purpose against which he knew that it would be madness for him to fight. Bram had more than the bad man's ordinary drop on him. In his wolves he possessed not only an advantage but a certainty. If Philip had doubted this, as he waited for another moment with the muzzle of his revolver close to the opening, this uncertainty was swept away by the appearance thirty feet in front of his tunnel of three of Bram's wolves. They were giants of their kind, and as the three faced his refuge he could see the snarling gleam of their long fangs. A fourth and a fifth joined them, and after that they came within his vision in twos and threes until a score of them were huddled straight in front of him. They were restless and whining, and the snap of their jaws was like the clicking of castanets. He caught the glare of twenty pairs of eyes fastened on his retreat and involuntarily he shrank back that they might not see him. He knew that it was Bram who was holding them back, and yet he had heard no word, no command. Even as he stared a long snakelike shadow uncurled itself swiftly in the air and the twenty foot lash of Bram's caribou-gut whip cracked viciously over the heads of the pack. At the warning of the whip the horde of beasts scattered, and Bram's voice came again.

"M'sieu—ze revolv'— ze knife—or I loose ze wolve—"

The words were scarcely out of his mouth when Philip's revolver flew through the opening and dropped in the snow.

"There it is, old man," announced Philip. "And here comes the knife."

His sheath-knife followed the revolver.

"Shall I throw out my bed?" he asked.

He was making a tremendous effort to appear cheerful. But he could not forget that last night he had shot at Bram, and that it was not at all unreasonable to suppose that Bram might knock his brains out when he stuck his head out of the hole. The fact that Bram made no answer to his question about the bed did not add to his assurance. He repeated the question, louder than before, and still there was no answer. In the face of his perplexity he could not repress a grim chuckle as he rolled up his blankets. What a report he would have for the Department—if he lived to make it! On paper there would be a good deal of comedy about it—this burrowing oneself up like a hibernating woodchuck, and then being invited out to breakfast by a man with a club and a pack of brutes with fangs that had gleamed at him like ivory stilettos. He had guessed at the club, and a moment later as he thrust his sleeping-bag out through the opening he saw that it was quite obviously a correct one. Bram was possessing himself of the revolver and the knife. In the same hand he held his whip and a club.

Seizing the opportunity, Philip followed his bed quickly, and when Bram faced him he was standing on his feet outside the drift.

"Morning, Bram!"

His greeting was drowned in a chorus of fierce snarls that

made his blood curdle even as he tried to hide from Bram any visible betrayal of the fact that every nerve up and down his spine was pricking him like a pin. From Bram's throat there shot forth at the pack a sudden sharp clack of Eskimo, and with it the long whip snapped in their faces again.

Then he looked steadily at his prisoner. For the first time Philip saw the look which he dreaded darkening his face. A greenish fire burned in the strange eyes. The thick lips were set tightly, the flat nose seemed flatter, and with a shiver Philip noticed Bram's huge, naked hand gripping his club until the cords stood out like babiche thongs under the skin. In that moment he was ready to kill. A wrong word, a wrong act, and Philip knew that the end was inevitable.

In the same thick guttural voice which he used in his halfbreed patois he demanded,

"Why you shoot—las' night?"

"Because I wanted to talk with you, Bram," replied Philip calmly. "I didn't shoot to hit you. I fired over your head."

"You want—talk," said Bram, speaking as if each word cost him a certain amount of effort. "Why—talk?"

"I wanted to ask you why it was that you killed a man down in the God's Lake country."

The words were out before Philip could stop them. A growl rose in Bram's chest. It was like the growl of a beast. The greenish fire in his eyes grew brighter.

"Ze poleece," he said. "Ka, ze poleece—like kam from Churchill an' ze wolve keel!"

Philip's hand was fumbling in his pocket. The wolves were behind him and he dared not turn to look. It was their ominous silence that filled him with dread. They were waiting—watching—their animal instinct telling them that the command for which they yearned was already trembling on the thick lips of their master. The revolver and the knife dropped from Bram's hand. He held only the whip and the club.

Philip drew forth the wallet.

"You lost something—when you camped that night near Pierre Breault's cabin," he said, and his own voice seemed strange and thick to him. "I've followed you—to give it back. I could have killed you if I had wanted to—when I fired over your head. But I wanted to stop you. I wanted to give you—this."

He held out to Bram the golden snare.

CHAPTER VIII

IT must have been fully half a minute that Bram stood like a living creature turned suddenly into dead stone. His eyes had left Philip's face and were fixed on the woven tress of shining hair. For the first time his thick lips had fallen agape. He did not seem to breathe. At the end of the thirty seconds his hand unclenched from about the whip and the club and they fell into the snow. Slowly, his eyes still fixed on the snare as if it held for him an overpowering fascination, he advanced a step, and then another, until he reached out and took from Philip the thing which he held. He uttered no word. But from his eyes there disappeared the greenish fire. The lines in his heavy face softened and his thick lips lost some of their cruelty as he held up the snare before his eyes so that the light played on its sheen of gold. It was then that Philip saw that which must have meant a smile in Bram's face.

Still this strange man made no spoken sound as he coiled the silken thread around one of his great fingers and then placed it somewhere inside his coat. He seemed, all at once, utterly oblivious of Philip's presence. He picked up the revolver, gazed heavily at it for a moment, and with a grunt which must have reflected his mental decision hurled it far out over the plain. Instantly the wolves were after it in a mad rush. The knife followed the revolver; and after that, as coolly as though breaking firewood, the giant went to Philip's rifle, braced it across his knee, and with a single effort snapped the stock off close to the barrel.

"The devil!" growled Philip.

He felt a surge of anger rise in him, and for an instant the inclination to fling himself at Bram in the defense of his property. If he had been helpless a few minutes before, he was utterly so now. In the same breath it flashed upon him that Bram's activity in the destruction of his weapons meant that his life was spared, at least for the present. Otherwise Bram would not be taking these precautions.

The futility of speech kept his own lips closed. At last Bram looked at him, and pointed to his snowshoes where he had placed them last night against the snow dune. His invitation for Philip to prepare himself for travel was accompanied by nothing more than a grunt.

The wolves were returning, sneaking in watchfully and alert. Bram greeted them with the snap of his whip, and when Philip was ready motioned him to lead the way into the north. Half a dozen paces behind Philip followed Bram, and twice that distance behind the outlaw came the pack. Now that his senses were readjusting themselves and his pulse beating more evenly Philip began to take stock of the situation. It was, first of all, quite evident that Bram had not accepted him as a traveling companion, but as a prisoner; and he was equally convinced that the golden snare had at the last moment served in some mysterious way to save his life.

It was not long before he saw how Bram had out-generaled him. Two miles beyond the big drift they came upon the outlaw's huge sledge, from which Bram and his wolves had made a wide circle in order to stalk him from behind. The fact puzzled him. Evidently Bram had expected his unknown enemy to pursue him, and had employed his strategy accordingly. Why, then, had he not attacked him the night of the caribou kill? He watched Bram as he got the pack into harness. The wolves obeyed him like dogs. He could perceive among them a strange comradeship, even an affection, for the man-monster who was their master. Bram spoke to them entirely in Eskimo—and the sound of it was like the rapid *clack-clack-clack* of dry bones striking together. It was weirdly different from the thick and guttural tones Bram used in speaking Chippewyan, the halfbreed patois.

Again Philip made an effort to induce Bram to break his oppressive silence. With a suggestive gesture and a hunch of his shoulders he nodded toward the pack, just as they were about to start.

"If you thought I tried to kill you night before why didn't you set your wolves after me, Bram—as you did those other two over on the Barren north of Kasba Lake? Why did you wait this morning? And where—where in God's name are we going?"

Bram stretched out an arm.

"There!"

It was the one question he answered, and he pointed straight as the needle of a compass into the north. And then, as if his crude sense of humor had been touched by the other thing Philip had asked he burst into a laugh. It made one shudder to see laughter in a face like Bram's. It transformed his countenance from mere ugliness into one of the leering gargoyles carven under the cornices of ancient buildings. It was this laugh heard almost at Bram's elbow, that made Philip suddenly grip hard at a new understanding—the laugh and the look in Bram's eyes. It set him throbbing, and filled him all at once with the desire to seize his companion by his great shoulders and shake speech from his thick lips. In that moment, even before the laughter had gone from Bram's face, he thought again of Pelletier. Pelletier must have been like this in those terrible days when he scribbled the random

thoughts of a half-mad man on his cabin door.

Bram was not yet mad. And yet he was fighting the thing that had killed Pelletier. Loneliness. The fate forced upon him by the law because he had killed a man.

His face was again heavy and unemotional when with a gesture he made Philip understand that he was to ride on the sledge. Bram himself went to the head of the pack. At the sharp clack of his Eskimo the wolves strained in their traces. Another moment and they were off, with Bram in the lead.

Philip was amazed at the pace set by the master of the pack. With head and shoulders hunched low he set off in huge swinging strides that kept the team on a steady trot behind him. They must have traveled eight miles an hour. For few minutes Philip could not keep his eyes from Bram and the gray backs of the wolves. They fascinated him, and at the same time the sight of them—straining on ahead of him into a voiceless and empty world—filled him with a strange and overwhelming compassion. He saw in them the brotherhood of man and beast. It was splendid. It was epic. And to this the Law had driven them!

His eyes began to take in the sledge then. On it was a roll of bear skins—Bram's blankets. One was the skin of a polar bear. Near these skins were the haunches of caribou meat, and so close to him that he might have reached out and touched it was Bram's club. At the side of the club lay a rifle. It was of the old breech-loading, single-shot type, and Philip wondered why Bram had destroyed his own modern weapon instead of keeping it in place of this ancient Company relic. It also made him think of night before last, when he had chosen for his refuge a tree out in the starlight.

The club, even more than the rifle, bore marks of use. It was of birch, and three feet in length. Where Bram's hand gripped it the wood was worn smooth and dark as mahogany. In many places the striking end of the club was dented as though it had suffered the impact of tremendous blows, and it was discolored by suggestive stains. There was no sign of cooking utensils and no evidence of any other food but the caribou flesh. On the rear of the sledge was a huge bundle of pitch-soaked spruce tied with babiche, and out of this stuck the crude handle of an ax.

Of these things the gun and the white bear skin impressed Philip most. He had only to lean forward a little to reach the rifle, and the thought, that he could scarcely miss the broad back of the man ahead of him struck him all at once with a sort of mental shock. Bram had evidently forgotten the weapon, or was utterly confident in the protection of the pack. Or—had he faith in his prisoner? It was this last question that Philip would liked to have answered in the affirmative. He had no desire to harm Bram. He had even a less desire to escape him. He had forgotten, so far as his personal intentions were concerned, that he was an agent of the Law—under oath to bring in to Divisional Headquarters Bram's body dead or alive. Since night before last Bram had ceased to be a criminal for him. He was like Pelletier, and through him he was entering upon a strange adventure which held for him already the thrill and suspense of an anticipation which he had never experienced in the game of manhunting.

Had the golden snare been taken from the equation—had he not felt the thrill of it in his fingers and looked upon the warm fires of it as it lay unbound on Pierre Breault's table, his present relation with Bram Johnson he would have considered as a purely physical condition, and he might then have accepted the presence of the rifle there within his reach as a direct invitation from Providence.

As it was, he knew that the master of the wolves was speeding swiftly to the source of the golden snare. From the moment he had seen the strange transformation it had worked in Bram that belief within him had become positive. And now, as his eyes turned from the inspection of sledge to Bram and his wolves, he wondered where the trail was taking him. Was it possible that Bram was striking straight north for Coronation Gulf and the Eskimo? He had noted that the polar bear skin was only slightly worn—that it had not long been taken from the back of the animal that had worn it. He recalled what he could remember of his geography. Their course, if it continued in the direction Bram was now heading, would take them east of the Great Slave and the Great Bear, and they would hit the Artic somewhere between Melville Sound and the Coppermine River. It was a good five hundred miles to the Eskimo settlements there. Bram and his wolves could make it in ten days, possibly in eight.

If his guess was correct, and Coronation Gulf was Bram's goal, he had found at least one possible explanation for the tress of golden hair.

The girl or woman to whom it had belonged had come into the north aboard a whaling ship. Probably she was the daughter or the wife of the master. The ship had been lost in the ice—she had been saved by the Eskimo—and she was among them now, with other white men. Philip pictured it all vividly. It was unpleasant—horrible. The theory of other white men being with her he was conscious of forcing upon himself to offset the more reasonable supposition that, as in the case of the golden snare, she belonged to Bram. He tried to free himself of that thought, but it clung to him with a tenaciousness that oppressed him with a grim and

ugly foreboding. What a monstrous fate for a woman! He
shivered. For a few moments every instinct in his body
fought to assure him that such a thing could not happen. And
yet he knew that it could happen. A woman up there—with
Bram! A woman with hair like spun gold—and that giant
half-mad enormity of a man!

He clenched his hands at the picture his excited brain
was painting for him. He wanted to jump from the sledge,
overtake Bram, and demand the truth from him. He was
calm enough to realize the absurdity of such action. Upon
his own strategy depended now whatever answer he might
make to the message chance had sent to him through the
golden snare.

For an hour he marked Bram's course by his compass. It
was straight north. Than Bram changed the manner of his
progress by riding in a standing position behind Philip. With
his long whip he urged on the pack until they were galloping
over the frozen level of the plain at a speed that must have
exceeded ten miles an hour. A dozen times Philip made
efforts at conversation. Not a word did he get from Bram in
reply. Again and again the outlaw shouted to his wolves in
Eskimo; he cracked his whip, he flung his great arms over
his head, and twice there rolled out of his chest deep peals
of strange laughter. They had been traveling more than two
hours when he gave voice to a sudden command that stopped
the pack and at a second command—a staccato of shrill
Eskimo accompanied by the lash of his whip—the panting
wolves sank upon their bellies in the snow.

Philip jumped from the sledge, and Bram went immediately
to the gun. He did not touch it, but dropped on his knees and
examined it closely. Then he rose to his feet and looked at
Philip, and there was no sign of madness in his heavy face

as he said,

"You no touch ze gun, m'sieu. Why you no shoot when I am there—at head of pack?"

The calmness and directness with which Bram put the question after his long and unaccountable silence surprised Philip.

"For the same reason you didn't kill me when I was asleep, I guess," he said. Suddenly he reached out and caught Bram's arm. "Why the devil don't you come across?" he demanded. "Why don't you talk? I'm not after you—now. The Police think you are dead, and I don't believe I'd tip them off even if I had a chance. Why not be human? Where are we going? And what in thunder —"

He did not finish. To his amazement Bram flung back his head, opened his great mouth, and laughed. It was not a taunting laugh. There was no humor in it. The thing seemed beyond the control of even Bram himself, and Philip stood like one paralyzed as his companion turned quickly to the sledge and returned in a moment with the gun. Under Philip's eyes he opened the breech. The chamber was empty. Bram had placed in his way a temptation—to test him!

There was saneness in that stratagem—and yet as Philip looked at the man now his last doubt was gone. Bram Johnson was hovering on the borderland of madness.

Replacing the gun on the sledge, Bram began hacking off chunks of the caribou flesh with a big knife. Evidently he had decided that it was time for himself and his pack to breakfast. To each of the wolves he gave a portion, after which he seated himself on the sledge and began devouring a slice of the raw meat. He had left the blade of his knife buried in the carcass—an invitation for Philip to help himself. Philip seated himself near Bram and opened his pack. Purposely he began placing his food between them, so that the other might help himself if he so desired. Bram's jaws ceased their crunching. For a moment Philip did not look up. When he did he was startled. Bram's eyes were blazing with a red fire. He was staring at the cooked food.

Never had Philip seen such a look in a human face before.

He reached out and seized a chunk of bannock, and was about to bite into it when with the snarl of a wild beast Bram dropped his meat and was at him. Before Philip could raise an arm in defense his enemy had him by the throat. Back over the sledge they went. Philip scarcely knew how it happened—but in another moment the giant had hurled him clean over his head and he struck the frozen plain with a shock that stunned him. When he staggered to his feet, expecting a final assault that would end him, Bram was kneeling beside his pack. A mumbling and incoherent jargon of sound issued from his thick lips as he took stock of Philip's supplies. Of Philip himself he seemed now utterly oblivious. Still mumbling, he dragged the pile of bear skins from the sledge, unrolled them, and revealed a worn and tattered dunnage bag. At first Philip thought this bag was empty. Then Bram drew from it a few small packages, some of them done up in paper and others in bark. Only one of these did Philip recognize—a half pound package of tea such as the Hudson's Bay Company offers in barter at its stores. Into the dunnage bag Bram now put Philip's supplies, even to the last crumb of bannock, and then returned the articles he had taken out, after which he rolled the bag up in the bear skins and replaced the skins on the sledge.

After that, still mumbling, and still paying no attention to Philip, he reseated himself on the edge of the sledge and finished his breakfast of raw meat.

"The poor devil!" mumbled Philip.

The words were out of his mouth before he realized that he had spoken them. He was still a little dazed by the shock of Bram's assault, but it was impossible for him to bear malice or thought of vengeance. In Bram's face, as he had covetously piled up the different articles of food, he had seen the terrible glare of starvation—and yet he had not eaten a mouthful. He had stored the food away, and Philip knew it was as much as his life was worth to contend its ownership.

Again Bram seemed to be unconscious of his presence, but when Philip went to the meat and began carving himself off a slice the wolf-man's eyes shot in his direction just once. Purposely he stood in front of Bram as he ate the raw steak, feigning a greater relish than he actually enjoyed in consuming his uncooked meal. Bram did not wait for him to finish. No sooner had he swallowed the last of his own breakfast than he was on his feet giving sharp commands to the pack. Instantly the wolves were alert in their traces. Philip took his former position on the sledge, with Bram behind him.

Never in all the years afterward did he forget that day. As the hours passed it seemed to him that neither man nor beast could very long stand the strain endured by Bram and his wolves. At times Bram rode on the sledge for short distances, but for the most part he was running behind, or at the head of the pack. For the pack there was no rest. Hour after hour it surged steadily onward over the endless plain, and whenever the wolves sagged for a moment in their traces Bram's whip snapped over their gray backs and his voice rang out in fierce exhortation. So hard was the frozen crust of the Barren that snowshoes were no longer necessary, and half a dozen times Philip left the sledge and ran with the wolf-man and his pack until he was winded. Twice he ran shoulder to shoulder with Bram.

It was in the middle of the afternoon that his compass told him they were no longer traveling north—but almost due west. Every quarter of an hour after that he looked at his compass. And always the course was west.

He was convinced that some unusual excitement was urging Bram on, and he was equally certain this excitement had taken possession of him from the moment he had found the food in his pack. Again and again he heard the strange giant mumbling incoherently to himself, but not once did Bram utter a word that he could understand.

The gray world about them was darkening when at last they stopped.

And now, strangely as before, Bram seemed for a few moments to turn into a sane man.

He pointed to the bundle of fuel, and as casually as though he had been conversing with him all the day he said to Philip:

"A fire, m'sieu."

The wolves had dropped in their traces, their great shaggy heads stretched out between their paws in utter exhaustion, and Bram went slowly down the line speaking to each one in turn. After that he fell again into his stolid silence. From the bear skins he produced a kettle, filled it with snow, and hung it over the pile of fagots to which Philip was touching a match. Philip's tea pail he employed in the same way.

"How far have we come, Bram?" Philip asked.

"Fift' mile, m'sieu," answered Bram without hesitation.

"And how much farther have we to go?"

Bram grunted. His face became more stolid. In his hand he was holding the big knife with which he cut the caribou meat. He was staring at it. From the knife he looked at Philip.

"I keel ze man at God's Lake because he steal ze knife—an' call me lie. I keel heem—lak that!" and he snatched up a stick and broke it into two pieces.

His weird laugh followed the words. He went to the meat and began carving off chunks for the pack, and for a long time after that one would have thought that he was dumb. Philip made greater effort than ever to rouse him into speech. He laughed, and whistled, and once tried the experiment of singing a snatch of the Caribou Song which he knew that Bram must have heard many times before. As he roasted his steak over the fire he talked about the Barren, and the great herd of caribou he had seen farther east; he asked Bram questions about the weather, the wolves, and the country farther north and west. More than once he was certain that Bram was listening intently, but nothing more than an occasional grunt was his response.

For an hour after they had finshed their supper they continued to melt snow for drinking water for themselves and the wolves. Night shut them in, and in the glow of the fire Bram scooped a hollow in the snow for a bed, and tilted the big sledge over it as a roof. Philip made himself as comfortable as he could with his sleeping bag, using his tent as an additional protection. The fire went out. Bram's heavy breathing told Philip that the wolf-man was soon asleep. It was a long time before he felt a drowsiness creeping over himself.

Later he was awakened by a heavy grasp on his arm, and roused himself to hear Bram's voice close over him.

"Get up, m'sieu."

It was so dark he could not see Bram when he got on

his feet, but he could hear him a moment later among the wolves, and knew that he was making ready to travel. When his sleeping-bag and tent were on the sledge he struck a match and looked at his watch. It was less than a quarter of an hour after midnight.

For two hours Bram led his pack straight into the west. The night cleared after that, and as the stars grew brighter and more numerous in the sky the plain was lighted up on all sides of them, as on the night when Philip had first seen Bram. By lighting an occasional match Philip continued to keep a record of direction and time. It was three o'clock, and they were still traveling west, when to his surprise they struck a small patch of timber. The clump of stunted and windsnarled spruce covered no more than half an acre, but it was conclusive evidence they were again approaching a timber-line.

From the patch of spruce Bram struck due north, and for another hour their trail was over the white Barren. Soon after this they came to a fringe of scattered timber which grew steadily heavier and deeper as they entered into it. They must have penetrated eight or ten miles into the forest before the dawn came. And in that dawn, gray and gloomy, they came suddenly upon a cabin.

Philip's heart gave a jump. Here, at last, would the mystery of the golden snare be solved. This was his first thought. But as they drew nearer, and stopped at the threshold of the door, he felt sweep over him an utter disappointment. There was no life here. No smoke came from the chimney and the door was almost buried in a huge drift of snow. His thoughts were cut short by the crack of Bram's whip. The wolves swept onward and Bram's insane laugh sent a weird and shuddering echo through the forest.

From the time they left behind them the lifeless and snow-smothered cabin Philip lost account of time and direction. He believed that Bram was nearing the end of his trail. The wolves were dead tired. The wolf-man himself was lagging, and since midnight had ridden more frequently on the sledge. Still he drove on, and Philip searched with increasing eagerness the trail ahead of them.

It was eight o'clock—two hours after they had passed the cabin—when they came to the edge of a clearing in the center of which was a second cabin. Here at a glance Philip saw there was life. A thin spiral of smoke was rising from the chimney. He could see only the roof of the log structure, for it was entirely shut in by a circular steeple of saplings six feet high.

Twenty paces from where Bram stopped his team was the gate of the stockade. Bram went to it, thrust his arm through a hole even with his shoulders, and a moment later the gate swung inward. For perhaps a space of twenty seconds he looked steadily at Philip, and for the first time Philip observed the remarkable change that had come into his face. It was no longer a face of almost brutish impassiveness. There was a strange glow in his eyes. His thick lips were, parted as if on the point of speech, and he was breathing with a quickness which did not come of physical exertion. Philip did not move or speak. Behind him he heard the restless whine of the wolves. He kept his eyes on Bram, and as he saw the look of joy and anticipation deepening in the wolf-man's face the appalling thought of what it meant sickened him. He clenched his hands. Bram did not see the act. He was looking again toward the cabin and at the spiral of smoke rising out of the chimney.

Then he faced Philip, and said,

"M'sieu, you go to ze cabin."

He held the gate open, and Philip entered. He paused to make certain of Bram's intention. The wolf-man swept an arm about the enclosure.

"In ze pit I loose ze wolve, m'sieu."

Philip understood. The stockade enclosure was Bram's wolf-pit, and Bram meant that he should reach the cabin before he gave the pack the freedom of the corral. He tried to conceal the excitement in his face as he turned toward the cabin. From the gate to the door ran a path worn by many footprints, and his heart beat faster as he noted the smallness of the moccasin tracks. Even then his mind fought against the possibility of the thing. Probably it was an Indian woman who lived with Bram, or an Eskimo girl he had brought down from the north.

He made no sound as he approached the door. He did not knock, but opened it and entered, as Bram had invited him to do.

From the gate Bram watched the cabin door as it closed behind him, and then he threw back his head and such a laugh of triumph came from his lips that even the tired beasts behind him pricked up their ears and listened.

And Philip, in that same moment, had solved the mystery of the golden snare.

CHAPTER IX

PHILIP had entered Bram Johnson's cabin from the west. Out of the east the pale fire of the winter sun seemed to concentrate itself on the one window of Bram's habitation, and flooded the opposite partition. In this partition there was a doorway, and in the doorway stood a girl.

She was standing full in the light that came through the window when Philip saw her. His first impression was that she was clouded in the same wonderful hair that had gone into the making of the golden snare. It billowed over her arms and breast to her hips, aflame with the living fires of the reflected sun. His second impression was that his entrance had interrupted her while she was dressing and that she was benumbed with astonishment as she stared at him. He caught the white gleam of her bare shoulders under her hair. And then, with a shock he saw what was in her face.

It turned his blood cold. It was the look of a soul that had been tortured. Agony and doubt burned in the eyes that were looking at him. He had never seen such eyes. They were like violet amethysts. Her face was dead white. It was beautiful. And she was young. She was not over twenty, it flashed upon him—but she had gone through a hell.

"Dont let me alarm you," he said, speaking gently. "I am Philip Raine of the Royal Northwest Mounted Police."

It did not surprise him that she made no answer. As plainly as if she had spoken it he had in those few swift moments read the story in her face. His heart choked him as he waited for her lips to move. It was a mystery to him afterward why he accepted the situation so utterly as he stood there. He had no question to ask, and there was no doubt in his mind. He knew that he would kill Bram Johnson when the moment arrived.

The girl had not seemed to breathe, but now she drew in her breath in a great gasp. He could see the sudden throb of her breast under her hair, but the frightened light did not leave her eyes even when he repeated the words he had spoken. Suddenly she ran to the window, and Philip saw the grip of her hands at the sill as she looked out. Through the gate Bram was driving his wolves. When she faced him again, her eyes had in them the look of a creature threatened by a whip. It amazed and startled him. As he advanced a step she cringed back from him. It struck him then that her face was like the face of an angel—filled with a mad horror. She reached out her bare arms to hold him back, and a strange pleading cry came from her lips.

The cry stopped him like a shot. He knew that she had spoken to him. And yet he had not understood! He tore open his coat and the sunlight fell on his bronze insignia of the Service. Its effect on her amazed him even more than had her sudden fear of him. It occurred to him suddenly that with a two weeks ragged growth of beard on his face he must look something like a beast himself. She had feared him, as she feared Bram, until she saw the badge.

"I am Philip Raine, of the Royal Northwest Mounted Police," he repeated again. "I have come up here especially to help you, if you need help. I could have got Bram farther back, but there was a reason why I didn't want him until I found his cabin. That reason was *you*. Why are you here with a madman and a murderer?"

She was watching him intently. Her eyes were on his lips, and into her face—white a few moments before—had risen swifly a flush of color. He saw the dread die out of her eyes in a new and dazzling excitement. Outside they could hear Bram. The girl turned again and looked through the window. Then she began talking, swiftly and eagerly, in a language that was as strange to Philip as the mystery of her presence in Bram Johnson's cabin. She knew that he could not understand, and suddenly she came up close to him and put a finger to his lips, and then to her own, and shook her head. He could fairly feel the throb of her excitement. The astounding truth held him dumb. She was trying to make him comprehend something—in a language which he had never heard before in all his life. He stared at her—like an idiot he told himself afterward.

And then the shuffle of Bram's heavy feet sounded just outside the door. Instantly the old light leapt into the girls eyes. Before the door could open she had darted into the room from which she had first appeared, her hair floating about her in a golden cloud as she ran.

The door opened, and Bram entered. At his heels, beyond the threshold, Philip caught a glimpse of the pack glaring hungrily into the cabin. Bram was burdened under the load he had brought from the sledge. He dropped it to the floor, and without looking at Philip his eyes fastened themselves on the door to the inner room.

They stood there for a full minute, Bram as if hypnotized by the door, and Philip with his eyes on Bram. Neither moved, and neither made a sound. A curtain had dropped over the entrance to the inner room, and beyond that they could hear the girl moving about. A dozen emotions were fighting in Philip. If he had possessed a weapon he would have ended the matter with Bram then, for the light that was burning like a strange flame in the wolf-man's eyes convinced him that he had guessed the truth. Bare-handed he was no match for the giant madman. For the first time he let his glance travel cautiously about the room. Near the stove was a pile of firewood. A stick of this would do—when the opportunity came.

And then, in a way that made him almost cry out, every nerve in his body was startled. The girl appeared in the doorway, a smile on her lips and her eyes shining radiantly—*straight at Bram!* She partly held out her arms, and began talking. She seemed utterly oblivious of Philip's presence. Not a word that she uttered could he understand. It was not Cree or Chippewyan or Eskimo. It was not French or German or any tongue that he had ever heard. Her voice was pure and soft. It trebled a little, and she was breathing quickly. But the look in her face that had at first horrified him was no longer there. She had braided her hair and had coiled the shining strands on the crown of her head, and the coloring in her face was like that of a rare painting. In these astounding moments he knew that such color and such hair did not go with any race that had ever bred in the northland. From her face, even as her lips spoke, he looked at Bram. The wolf-man was transfigured. His strange eyes were shining, his heavy face was filled with a dog-like joy, and his thick lips moved as if he was repeating to himself what the girl was saying.

Was it possible that he understood her? Was the strange language in which she was speaking common between them? At first Philip thought that it must be so—and all the horrors of the situation that he had built up for himself fell about him in confusing disorder. The girl, as she stood there now, seemed glad that Bram had returned; and with a heart choking him with its suspense he waited for Bram to speak, and act.

When the girl ceased speaking the wolf-man's response

came in a guttural cry that was like a paean of triumph. He dropped on his knees beside the dunnage bag and mumbling thickly as he worked he began emptying its contents upon the floor.

Philip looked at the girl. She was looking at him now. Her hands were clutched at her breast, and in her face and attitude there was a wordless entreaty for him to understand. The truth came to him like a flash. For some reason she had forced herself to appear that way to the wolf-man. She had forced herself to smile, forced the look of gladness into her face, and the words from her lips. And now she was trying to tell him what it meant, and pointing to Bram as he knelt with his huge head and shoulders bent over the dunnage bag on the floor she exclaimed in a low tense voice:

"*Tossi—tossi—han er tossi!*"

It was useless. He could not understand, and it was impossible for him to hide the bewilderment in his face. All at once an inspiration came to him. Bram's back was toward him, and he pointed to the sticks of firewood. His pantomime was clear. Should he knock the wolf-man's brains out as he knelt there?

He could see that his question sent a thrill of alarm through her. She shook her head. Her lips formed strange words, and looking again at Bram she repeated, "*Tossi—tossi—han er tossi!*" She clasped her hands suddenly to her head then. Her slim fingers buried themselves in the thick braids of her hair. Her eyes dilated—and suddenly understanding flashed upon him. She was telling him what he already knew—that Bram Johnson was mad, and he repeated after her the "*Tossi—tossi,*" tapping his forehead suggestively, and nodding at Bram. Yes, that was it. He could see it in the quick intake of her breath and the sudden expression of relief that swept over her face. She had been afraid he would attack the wolf-man. And now she was glad that he understood he was not to harm him.

If the situation had seemed fairly clear to him a few minutes before it had become more deeply mysterious than ever now. Even as the wolf-man rose from his knees, still mumbling to himself in incoherent exultation, the great and unanswerable question pounded in Philip's brain: "Who was this girl, and what was she to Bram Johnson—the crazed outlaw whom she feared and yet whom she did not wish him to harm?"

And then he saw her staring at the things which Bram had sorted out on the floor. In her eyes was hunger. It was a living, palpitant part of her now as she stared at the things which Bram had taken from the dunnage bag—as surely as Bram's madness was a part of him. As Philip watched her he knew that slowly the curtain was rising on the tragedy of the golden snare. In a way the look that he saw in her face shocked him more than anything that he had seen in Bram's. It was as if, in fact, a curtain had lifted before his eyes revealing to him an unbelievable truth, and something of the hell through which she had gone. She was hungry—for something that was *not flesh!* Swiftly the thought flashed upon him why the wolf-man had traveled so far to the south, and why he had attacked him for possession of his food supply. It was that he might bring these things to the girl. He knew that it was sex-pride that restrained the impulse that was pounding in every vein of her body. She wanted to fling herself down on her knees beside that pile of stuff—but she remembered him! Her eyes met his, and the shame of her confession swept in a crimson flood into her face. The feminine instinct told her that she had betrayed herself—like an animal, and that he must have seen in her for a moment something that was almost like Bram's own madness.

CHAPTER X

UNTIL he felt the warm thrill of the girl's arm under his hand Philip did not realize the hazard he had taken. He turned suddenly to confront Bram. He would not have known then that the wolf-man was mad, and impulsively he reached out a hand.

"Bram, she's starving," he cried. "I know now why you wanted that stuff! But why didn't you tell me? Why don't you talk, and let me know who she is, and why she is here, and what you want me to do?" He waited, and Bram stared at him without a sound.

"I tell you I'm a friend," he went on. "I—"

He got no farther than that, for suddenly the cabin was filled with the madness of Bram's laugh. It was more terrible than out on the open Barren, or in the forest, and he felt the shudder of the girl at his side. Her face was close to his shoulder, and looking down he saw that it was white as death, but that even then she was trying to smile at Bram. And Bram continued to laugh—and as he laughed, his eyes blazing a greenish fire, he turned to the stove and began putting fuel into the fire. It was horrible. Bram's laugh—the girl's dead white face, *and her smile!* He no longer asked himself who she was, and why she was there. He was overwhelmed by the one appalling fact that she *was* here, and that the stricken soul crying out to him from the depths of those eyes that were like wonderful blue amethysts told him that Bram had made her pay the price. His muscles hardened as he looked at the huge form bending over the stove. It was a splendid opportunity. A single leap and he would be at the outlaw's throat. With that advantage, in open combat, the struggle would at least be equal.

The girl must have guessed what was in his mind, for suddenly her fingers were clutching at his arm and she was pulling him away from the wolf-man, speaking to him in the language which he could not understand. And then Bram turned from the stove, picked up a pail, and without looking at them left the cabin. They could hear his laugh as he joined the wolves.

Again Philip's conclusions topled down about him like a thing made of blocks. During the next few moments he knew that the girl was telling him that Bram had not harmed her. She seemed almost hysterically anxious to make him understand this, and at last, seizing him by the hand, she drew him into the room beyond the curtained door. Her meaning was quite as plain as words. She was showing him what Bram had done for her. He had made her this separate room by running a partition across the cabin, and in addition to this he had built a small lean-to outside the main wall entered through a narrow door made of saplings that were still green. He noticed that the partition was also made of fresh timber. Except for the bunk built against the wall, a crude chair, a sapling table and half a dozen bear skins that carpeted the floor the room was empty. A few garments hung on the wall—a hood made of fur, a thick mackinaw coat belted at the waist with a red scarf, and something done up in a small bundle.

"I guess—I begin to get your meaning," he said, looking straight into her shining blue eyes. "You want to impress on me that I'm not to wring Bram Johnson's neck when his back is turned, or at any other time, and you want me to believe that he hasn't done you any harm. And yet you're afraid to the bottom of your soul. I know it. A little while ago your face was as white as chalk, and now—now—it's the prettiest face I've ever seen. Now, see here, little girl—"

It gave him a pleasant thrill to see the glow in her eyes and the eager poise of her slim, beautiful body as she listened to him.

"I'm licked," he went on, smiling frankly at her. "At least for the present. Maybe I've gone loony, like Bram, and don't realize it yet. I set out for a couple of Indians, and find a madman; and at the madman's cabin I find *you*, looking at first as though you were facing straight up against the door of—of—well, seeing that you can't understand I might as well say it—*of hell!* Now, if you weren't afraid of Bram, and if he hasn't hurt you, why did you look like that? I'm stumped. I repeat it—dead stumped. I'd give a million dollars if I could make Bram talk. I saw what was in his eyes. *You* saw it— and that pretty pink went out of your face so quick it seemed as though your heart must have stopped beating. And yet you're trying to tell me he hasn't harmed you. My God—I wish I could believe it!"

In her face he saw the reflection of the change that must have come suddenly into his own.

"You're a good fifteen hundred miles from any other human being with hair and eyes and color like yours," he continued, as though in speaking his thoughts aloud to her some ray of light might throw itself on the situation. "If you had something black about you. But you haven't. You're all gold—pink and white and gold. If Bram has another fit of talking he may tell me you came from the moon—that a *chasse-galere* crew brought you down out of space to keep house for him. Great Scott, can't you give me *some* sort of an idea of who you are and where you came from?"

He paused for an answer—and she smiled at him. There was something pathetically sweet in that smile. It brought a queer lump into his throat, and for a space he forgot Bram.

"You don't understand a cussed word of it, do you?" he said, taking her hand in both his own and holding it closely for a moment. "Not a word. But we're getting the drift of things—slowly. I know you've been here quite a while, and that morning, noon and night since the *chasse-galere* brought you down from the moon you've had nothing to put your little teeth into but meat. Probably without salt, too. I saw how you wanted to throw yourself down on that pile of stuff on the floor. Let's have breakfast!"

He led her into the outer room, and eagerly she set to work helping him gather the things from the floor. He felt that an overwhelming load had been lifted from his heart, and he continued to tell her about it while he hurried the preparation for the breakfast for which he knew she was hungering. He did not look at her too closely. All at once it had dawned upon him that her situation must be tremendously more embarrassing than his own. He felt, too, the tingle of a new excitement in his veins. It was a pleasurable sensation, something which he did not pause to analyze just at present. Only he knew that it was because she had told him as plainly as she could Bram had not harmed her.

"And if he *had* I guess you'd have let me smash his brains out when he was bending over the stove, wouldn't you?" He said, stirring the mess of desiccated potato he was warming in one of his kit-pans. He looked up to see her eyes shining at him, and her lips parted. She was delightfully pretty. He knew that every nerve in her body was straining to understand him. Her braid had slipped over her shoulder. It was as thick as his wrist, and partly undone. He had never dreamed that a woman's hair could hold such soft warm fires of velvety gold. Suddenly he straightened himself and tapped his chest, an inspiring thought leaping into his head.

"I am Philip Raine," he said. "Philip Raine—Philip Raine—Philip Raine—"

He repeated the name over and over again, pointing each time to himself. Instantly light flashed into her face. It was as if all at once they had broken through the barrier that had separated them. She repeated his name, slowly, clearly, smiling at him, and then with both hands at her breast, she said:

"*Celie Armin.*"

He wanted to jump over the stove and shake hands with her, but the potatoes were sizzling. Celie Armin! He repeated the name as he stirred the potatoes, and each time he spoke it she nodded. It was decidedly a French name—but half a minute's experiment with a few simple sentences of Pierre Breault's language convinced him that the girl understood no word of it.

Then he said again:

"Celie!"

Almost in the same breath she answered:

"Philip!"

Sounds outside the cabin announced the return of Bram. Following the snarl and whine of the pack came heavy footsteps, and the wolf-man entered. Philip did not turn his head toward the door. He did not look at first to see what effect Bram's return had on Celie Armin. He went on casually with his work. He even began to whistle; and then, after a final stir or two at the potatoes, he pointed to the pail in which the coffe was bubbling, and said:

"Turn the coffee, Celie. We're ready!"

He caught a glimpse of her face then. The excitement and color had partly died out of it. She took the pail of coffee and went with it to the the table.

Then Philip faced Bram.

The wolf-man was standing with his back to the door. He had not moved since entering, and he was staring at the scene before him in a dull, stupid sort of way. In one hand he carried a pail filled with water; in the other a frozen fish.

"Too late with the fish, Bram," said Philip. "We couldn't make the little lady wait. Besides, I think you've fed her on fish and meat until she is just about ready to die. Come to breakfast!"

He loaded a tin plate with hot potatoes, bannock-bread and rice that he had cooked before setting out on the Barren, and placed it before the girl. A second plate he prepared for Bram, and a third for himself. Bram had not moved. He still held the pail and the fish in his hands. Suddenly he lowered both to the floor with a growl that seemed to come from the bottom of his great chest, and came to the table. With one huge hand he seized Philip's arm. It was not a man's grip. There was apparently no effort in it, and yet it was a vise-like clutch that threatened to snap the bone. And all the time Bram's eyes were on the girl. He drew Philip back, released the terrible grip on his arm, and shoved the two extra plates of food to the girl. Then he faced Philip.

"We eat ze meat, m'sieu!"

Quietly and sanely he uttered the words. In his eyes and face there was no trace of madness. And then, even as Philip stared, the change came. The giant flung back his head and his wild, mad laugh rocked the cabin. Out in the corral the snarl and cry of the wolves gave a savage response to it.

It took a tremendous effort for Philip to keep a grip on himself. In that momentary flash of sanity Bram had shown a chivalry which must have struck deep home in the heart of the girl. There was a sort of triumph in her eyes when he looked at her. She knew now that he must understand fully what she had been trying to tell him. Bram, in his madness, had been good to her. Philip did not hesitate in the impulse of the moment. He caught Bram's hand and shook it. And Bram, his laugh dying away in a mumbling sound, seemed not to notice it. As Philip began preparing the fish the wolf-man took up a position against the farther wall, squatting Indian-fashion on his heels. He did not take his eyes from the girl until she had finished, and Philip brought him a half of the fried fish. He might as well have offered the fish to a wooden sphinx. Bram rose to his feet, mumbling softly, and taking what was left of one of the two caribou quarters he again left the cabin.

His mad laugh and the snarling outcry of the wolves came to them a moment later.

CHAPTER XI

SCARCELY had the door closed when Celie Armin ran to Philip and pulled him to the table. In the tense half hour of Bram's watchfulness she had eaten her own breakfast as if nothing unusual had happened; now she insisted on adding potatoes and bannock to Philip's fish, and turned him a cup of coffee.

"Bless your heart, you don't want to see me beat out of a breakfast, do you?" He looked up at her feeling all at once an immense desire to pull her head down to him and kiss her. "But you don't understand the situation, little girl. Now I've been eating this confounded bannock—he picked up a chunk of it to demonstrate his point—morning, noon and night until the sight of it makes me almost cry for one of mother's green cucumber pickles. I'm tired of it. Bram's fish is a treat. And this coffee, seeing that you have turned it in that way—"

She sat opposite him while he ate, and he had the chance of observing her closely while his meal progressed. It struck him that she was growing prettier each time that he looked at her, and he was more positive than ever that she was a stranger in the northland. Again he told himself that she was not more than twenty. Mentally he even went so far as to weigh her and would have gambled that she would not have tipped a scale five pounds one way or the other from a hundred and twenty. Some time he might have seen the kind of violet-blue that was in her eyes, but he could not remember it. She was lost—utterly lost at this far-end of the earth. She was no more a part of it than a crepe de chine ball dress or a bit of rose china. And there she was, sitting opposite him, a bewitching mystery for him to solve. And she *wanted* to be solved! He could see it in her eyes, and in the little beating throb at her throat. She was fighting, with him, to find a way; a way to tell him who she was, and why she was here, and what he must do for her.

Suddenly he thought of the golden snare. That, after all, he believed to be the real key to the mystery. He rose quickly from the table and drew the girl to the window. At the far end of the corral they could see Bram tossing chunks of meat to the horde of beasts that surrounded him. In a moment or two he had the satisfaction of seeing that his companion understood that he was directing her attention to the wolf-man and not the pack. Then he began unbraiding her hair. His fingers thrilled at the silken touch of it. He felt his face flushing hot under his beard, and he knew that her eyes were on him wonderingly. A small strand he divided into three parts and began weaving into a silken thread only a little larger than the wolf-man's snare. From the woven tress he pointed to Bram and in an instant her face lighted up with understanding.

She answered him in pantomime. Either she or Bram had cut the tress from her head that had gone into the making of the golden snare. And not only one tress, but several. There had been a number of golden snares. She bowed her head and showed him where strands as large as her little finger had been clipped in several places.

Philip almost groaned. She was telling him nothing new, except that there had been many snares instead of one.

He was on the point of speech when the look in her face held him silent. Her eyes glowed with a sudden excitement—a wild inspiration. She held out her hands until they nearly touched his breast.

"Philip Raine—*Amerika!*" she cried.

Then, pressing her hands to her own breast, she added

eagerly:

"Celie Armin—*Danmark!*"

"Denmark!" exclaimed Philip. "Is that it, little girl? You're from Denmark? Denmark?"

She nodded.

"*Kobenhavn—Danmark!*"

"Copenhagen, Denmark," he translated for himself. "Great Scott, Celie—we're *talking!* Celie Armin, from Copenhagen, Denmark! But how in Heaven's name did you get *here?*" He pointed to the floor under their feet and embraced the four walls of the cabin in a wide gesture of his arms. "How did you get *here?*"

Her next words thrilled him.

"*Kobenhavn—Muskvas—St. Petersburg—Rusland—Sibirien—Amerika.*"

"Copenhagen—Muskvas, whatever that is—St. Petersburg—Russia—Siberia—America," he repeated, staring at her incredulously. "Celie, if you love me, be reasonable! Do you expect me to believe that you came all the way from Denmark to this God-forsaken madman's cabin in the heart of the Canada Barrens by way of Russia and Siberia? *You!* I can't believe it. There's a mistake somewhere. Here—"

He thought of his pocket atlas, supplied by the department as a part of his service kit, and remembered that in the back of it was a small map of the world. In half a minute he had secured it and was holding the map under her eyes. Her little forefinger touched Copenhagen. Leaning over her shoulder, he felt her hair crumpling against his breast. He felt an insane desire to bury his face in it and hug her up close in his arms—for a single moment the question of whether she came from Copenhagen or the moon was irrelevant and of little consequence. He, at least had found her. He was digging her out of chaos, and he was filled with the joyous exultation of a triumphant discoverer—almost the thrill of ownership. He held his breath as he watched the little forefinger telling him its story on the map.

From Copenhagen it went to Moscow—which must have been *Muskvas*, and from there it trailed slowly to St. Petersburg and thence straight across Russia and Siberia to the Bering Sea.

"*Skunnert*," she said softly, and her finger came across to the green patch on the map which was Alaska.

It hesitated there. Evidently it was a question in her own mind where she had gone after that. At least she could not tell him on the map. And now, seeing that he was understanding her, she was becoming visibly excited. She pulled him to the window and pointed to the wolves. Alaska—and after that dogs and sledge. He nodded. He was jubilant. She was Celie Armin, of Copenhagen, Denmark, and had come to Alaska by way of Russia and Siberia—and after that had traveled by dog-train. But *why* had she come, and what had happened to make her the companion or prisoner of Bram Johnson? He knew she was trying to tell him. With her back to the window she talked to him again, gesturing with her hands, and almost sobbing under the stress of the emotion that possessed her. His elation turned swiftly to the old dread as he watched the change in her face. Apprehension—a grim certainty—gripped hold of him. Something terrible had happened to her—a thing that had racked her soul and that filled her eyes with the blaze of a strange terror as she struggled to make him understand. And then she broke down, and with a sobbing cry covered her face with her hands.

Out in the corral Philip heard Bram Johnson's laugh. It was a mockery—a challenge. In an instant every drop of blood in his body answered it in a surge of blind rage. He sprang to the stove, snatched up a length of firewood, and in another moment was at the door. As he opened it and ran out he heard Celie's wild appeal for him to stop. It was almost a scream. Before he had taken a dozen steps from the cabin he realized what the warning meant. The pack had seen him and from the end of the corral came rushing at him in a thick mass.

This time Bram Johnson's voice did not stop them. He saw Philip, and from the doorway Celie looked upon the scene while the blood froze in her veins. She screamed—and in the same breath came the wolf-mans laugh. Philip heard both as he swung the stick of firewood over his head and sent it hurling toward the pack. The chance accuracy of the throw gave him an instant's time in which to turn and make a dash for the cabin. It was Celie who slammed the door shut as he sprang through. Swift as a flash she shot the bolt, and there came the lunge of heavy bodies outside. They could hear the snapping of jaws and the snarling whine of the beasts. Philip had never seen a face whiter than the girl's had gone. She covered it with her hands, and he could see her trembling. A bit of a sob broke hysterically from her lips.

He knew of what she was thinking—the horrible thing she was hiding from her eyes It was plain enough to him now. Twenty seconds more and they would have had him. And then—

He drew in a deep breath and gently uncovered her face. Her hands shivered in his. And then a great throb of joy repaid him for his venture into the jaws of death as he saw the way in which her beautiful eyes were looking at him.

"Celie—my little mystery girl—I've discovered something," he cried huskily, holding her hands so tightly that it must have hurt her. "I'm almost glad that you can't understand me, for I wouldn't blame you for being afraid of a man who told you he loved you an hour or two after he first saw you. I love you. I've never wanted anything in all my life as I want you. And I must be careful and not let you know it, mustn't I? If I did, you'd think I was some kind of an animal-brute—like Bram. Wouldn't you?"

Bram's voice came in a sharp rattle of Eskimo outside. Philip could hear the snarling rebellion of the wolves as they slunk away from the cabin, and he drew Celie back from the door. Suddenly, she freed her hands, ran to the door and slipped back the wooden bolt as the wolf-man's hand fumbled at the latch. In a moment she was back at his side. When Bram entered every muscle in Philip's body was prepared for action. He was amazed at the wolf-man's unconcern. He was mumbling and chuckling to himself, as if amused at what he had seen. Celie's little fingers dug into Philip's arm and he saw in her eyes a tense, staring look that had not been there before. It was as if in Bram's face and his queer mumbling she had recognized something which was not apparent to him. Suddenly she left him and hurried into her room. During the few moments she was gone Bram did not look once at Philip. His mumbling was incessant. Perhaps a minute passed before the girl reappeared.

She went straight to Bram and before the wolf-man's eyes held a long, shining tress of hair!

Instantly the mumbling in Bram's throat ceased and he thrust out slowly a huge misshapen hand toward the golden strand. Philip felt his nerves stretching to the breaking point. With Bram the girl's hair was a fetich. A look of strange exultation crept over the giant's heavy features as his fingers clutched the golden offering. It almost drew a cry of warning from Philip. He saw the girl smiling in the face of a deadly peril—a danger of which she was apparently unconscious. Her hair still fell loose about her in a thick and shimmering glory. And *Bram's eyes were on it as he took the tress from her fingers!* Was it conceivable that this madman did not comprehend his power? Had the thought not yet burned its way into his thick brain that a treasure many times greater than that which she had doled out to him lay within the reach of his brute hands at any time he cared to reach out for it? And was it possible that the girl did not guess her danger as she stood there?

What she could see of his face must have been as pale as her own when she looked at him. She smiled, and nodded at Bram. The giant was turning slowly toward the window, and after a moment or two in which they could hear him mumbling softly he sat down cross-legged against the wall, divided the tress into three silken threads and began weaving them into a snare. The color was returning to Celie's face when Philip looked at her again. She told him with a gesture of her head and hands that she was going into her room for a time. He didn't blame her. The excitement had been rather unusual.

After she had gone he dug his shaving outfit out of his kit-bag. It included a mirror and the reflection he saw in this mirror fairly shocked him. No wonder the girl had been frightened at his first appearance. It took him half an hour to shave his face clean, and all that time Bram paid no attention to him but went on steadily at his task of weaving the golden snare. Celie did not reappear until the wolf-man had finished and was leaving the cabin. The first thing she noticed was the change in Philip's face. He saw the pleasure in her eyes and felt himself blushing.

From the window they watched Bram. He had called his wolves and was going with them to the gate. He carried his snowshoes and his long whip. He went through the gate first and one by one let his beasts out until ten of the twenty had followed him. The gate was closed then.

Celie turned to the table and Philip saw that she had brought from her room a pencil and a bit of paper. In a moment she held the paper out to him, a light of triumph in her face. At last they had found a way to talk. On the paper was a crude sketch of a caribou head. It meant that Bram had gone hunting.

And in going Bram had left a half of his blood-thirsty pack in the corral. There was no longer a doubt in Philip's mind. They were not the chance guests of this madman. They were prisoners.

CHAPTER XII

FOR a few minutes after the wolf-man and his hunters had gone from the corral Philip did not move from the window. He almost forgot that the girl was standing behind him. At no time since Pierre Breault had revealed the golden snare had the situation been more of an enigma to him than now. Was Bram Johnson actually mad—or was he playing a colossal sham? The question had unleashed itself in his brain with a suddenness that had startled him. Out of the past a voice came to him distinctly, and it said, "A madman never forgets!" It was the voice of a great alienist, a good friend of his, with whom he had discussed the sanity of a man whose crime had shocked the country. He knew that the words were true. Once possessed by an idea the madman will not forget it. It becomes an obsession with him—a part of his existence. In his warped brain a suspicion never dies. A fear will smolder everlastingly. A hatred lives steadily on.

If Bram Johnson was mad would he play the game as he was playing it now? He had almost killed Philip for possession of the food, that the girl might have the last crumb of it. Now, without a sign of the madman's caution, he had left it all within his reach again. A dozen times the flaming suspicion in his eyes had been replaced by a calm and stupid indifference. Was the suspicion real and the stupidity a clever dissimulation? And if dissimulation—why?

He was positive now that Bram had not harmed the girl in the way he had dreaded. Physical desire had played no part in the wolf-man's possession of her. Celie had made him understand that;—and yet in Bram's eyes he had caught a look now and then that was like the dumb worship of a beast.

Only once had that look been anything different—and that was when Celie had given him a tress of her hair. Even the suspicion roused in him then was gone now, for if passion and desire were smoldering in the wolf-man's breast he would not have brought a possible rival to the cabin, nor would he have left them alone together.

His mind worked swiftly as he stared unseeing out into the corral. He would no longer play the part of a pawn. Thus far Bram had held the whip hand. Now he would take if from him no matter what mysterious protestation the girl might make. The wolf-man had given him a dozen opportunities to deliver the blow that would make him a prisoner. He would not miss the next.

He faced Celie with the gleam of this determination in his eyes. She had been watching him intently and he believed that she had guessed a part of his thoughts. His first business was to take advantage of Bram's absence to search the cabin. He tried to make Celie understand what his intentions were as he began.

"You may have done this yourself," he told her. "No doubt you have. There probably isn't a corner you haven't looked into. But I have a hunch I may find something you missed—something interesting."

She followed him closely. He began at each wall and went over it carefully, looking for possible hiding places. Then he examined the floor for a loose sapling. At the end of half an hour his discoveries amounted to nothing. He gave an exclamation of satisfaction when under an old blanket in a dusty corner he found a Colt army revolver. But it was empty, and he found no cartridges. At last there was nothing left to search but the wolf-man's bunk. At the bottom of this he found what gave him his first real thrill—three of the silken snares made from Celie Armin's hair.

"We won't touch them," he said after a moment, replacing the bear skin that had covered them. "It's good etiquette up here not to disturb another man's cache and that's Bram's. I can't imagine any one but a madman doing that. And yet— "

He looked suddenly at Celie.

"Do you suppose he was afraid of *you?*" He asked her. "Is that why he doesn't leave even the butcher-knife in this shack? Was he afraid you might shoot him in his sleep if he left the temptation in your way?"

A commotion among the wolves drew him to the window. Two of the beasts were fighting. While his back was turned Celie entered her room and returned a moment or two later with a handful of loose bits of paper. The pack held Philip's attention. He wondered what chance he would have in an encounter with the beasts which Bram had left behind as a guard. Even if he killed Bram or made him a prisoner he would still have that horde of murderous brutes to deal with. If he could in some way induce the wolf-man to bring his rifle into the cabin the matter would be easy. With Bram out of the way he could shoot the wolves one by one from the window. Without a weapon their situation would be hopeless. The pack—with the exception of one huge, gaunt beast directly under the window—had swung around the end of the cabin out of his vision. The remaining wolf in spite of the excitement of battle was gnawing hungrily at a bone. Philip could hear the savage grind of its powerful jaws, and all at once the thought of how they might work out their salvation flashed upon him. They could starve the wolves! It would take a week, perhaps ten days, but with Bram out of the way and the pack helplessly imprisoned within the corral it could be done. His first impulse now was to impress on Celie the necessity of taking physical action against Bram.

The sound of his own name turned him from the window with a sudden thrill.

If the last few minutes had inspired an eagerness for action in his own mind he saw at a glance that something equally exciting had possessed Celie Armin. Spread out on the table were the bits of paper she had brought from her room, and, pointing to them, she again called him by name. That she was laboring under a new and unusual emotion impressed him immediately. He could see that she was fighting to restrain an impulse to pour out in words what would have been meaningless to him, and that she was telling him the bits of paper were to take the place of voice. For one swift moment as he advanced to the table the papers meant less to him than the fact that she had twice spoken his name. Her soft lips seemed to whisper it again as she pointed, and the look in her eyes and the poise of her body recalled to him vividly the picture of her as he had first seen her in the cabin. He looked at the bits of paper. There were fifteen or twenty pieces, and on each was sketched a picture.

He heard a low catch in Celie's breath as he bent over them, and his own pulse quickened. A glance was sufficient to show him that with the pictures Celie was trying to tell him what he wanted to know. They told her own story— who she was, why she was at Bram Johnson's cabin, and how she had come. This, at least, was the first thought that impressed him. He observed then that the bits of paper were soiled and worn as though they had been handled a great deal. He made no effort to restrain the exclamation that followed this discovery.

"You drew these pictures for Bram," he said, scanning

them more carefully. "That settles one thing. Bram doesn't know much more about you than I do. Ships, and dogs, and men—and fighting—a lot of fighting—and—"

His eyes stopped at one of the pictures and his heart gave a sudden excited thump. He picked up the bit of paper which had evidently been part of a small sack. Slowly he turned to the girl and met her eyes. She was trembling in her eagerness for him to understand.

"That is *you*," he said, tapping the central figure in the sketch, and nodding at her. You—with your hair down, and fighting a bunch of men who look as though they were about to beat your brains out with clubs! Now—what in God's name does it mean? And here's a ship up in the corner. That evidently came first. You landed from that ship, didn't you? From the ship—the ship—the ship—"

"*Skunnert!*" She cried softly, touching the ship with her finger. "*Skunnert—Sibirien!*"

"Schooner—Siberia," translated Philip. "It sounds mightily like that, Celie. Look here —" He opened his pocket atlas again at the map of the world. "Where did you start from, and where did you come ashore? If we can get at the beginning of the thing—"

She had bent her head over the crook of his arm, so that in her eager scrutiny of the map his lips for a moment or two touched the velvety softness of her hair. Again he felt the exquisite thrill of her touch, the throb of her body against him, the desire to take her in his arms and hold her there. And then she drew back a little, and her finger was once more tracing out its story on the map. The ship had started from the mouth of the Lena River, in Siberia, and had followed the coast to the blue space that marked the ocean above Alaska. And there the little finger paused, and with a hopeless gesture Celie intimated that was all she knew. From somewhere out of that blue patch the ship had touched the American shore. One after another she took up from the table the pieces of paper that carried on the picture-story from that point. It was, of course, a broken and disjointed story. But as it progressed every drop of blood in Philip's body was stirred by the thrill and mystery of it. Celie Armin had traveled from Denmark through Russia to the Lena River in Siberia, and from there a ship had brought her to the coast of North America. There had been a lot of fighting, the significance of which he could only guess at; and now, at the end, the girl drew for Philip another sketch in which a giant and a horde of beasts appeared. It was a picture of Bram and his wolves, and at last Philip understood why she did not want him to harm the wolf-man. Bram had saved her from the fate which the pictures only partly portrayed for him. He had brought her far south to his hidden stronghold, and for some reason which the pictures failed to disclose was keeping her a prisoner there.

Beyond these things Celie Armin was still a mystery. Why had she gone to Siberia? What had brought her to the barren Arctic coast of America? Who were the mysterious enemies from whom Bram the madman had saved her? And who—who—

He looked again at one of the pictures which he had partly crumpled in his hand. On it were sketched two people. One was a figure with her hair streaming down—Celie herself. The other was a man. The girl had pictured herself close in the embrace of this man's arms. Her own arms encircled the man's neck. From the picture Philip had looked at Celie, and the look he had seen in her eyes and face filled his heart with a leaden chill. It was more than hope that had flared up in his breast since he had entered Bram Johnson's cabin. And now that hope went suddenly out, and with its extinguishment he was oppressed by a deep and gloomy foreboding.

He went slowly to the window and looked out. The next moment Celie was startled by the sudden sharp cry that burst from his lips. Swiftly she ran to his side. He had dropped the paper. His hands were gripping the edge of the sill, and he was staring like one who could not believe his own eyes.

"Good God—look! Look at that!"

They had heard no sound outside the cabin during the last few minutes. Yet under their eyes, stretched out in the soiled and trampled snow, lay the wolf that a short time before had been gnawing a bone. The animal was stark dead. Not a muscle of its body moved. Its lips were drawn back, its jaws agape, and under the head was a growing smear of blood. It was not these things—not the fact but the *instrument* of death that held Philip's eyes. The huge wolf had been completely transfixed by a spear.

Instantly, Philip recognized it—the long, slender, javelin-like narwhal harpoon used by only one people in the world, the murderous little black-visaged Kogmollocks of Coronation Gulf and Wollaston Land.

He sprang suddenly back from the window, dragging Celie with him.

CHAPTER XIII

"KOGMOLLOCKS—the blackest-hearted little devils alive when it comes to trading wives and fighting," said Philip, a little ashamed of the suddenness with which he had jumped back from the window. "Excuse my abruptness, dear. But I'd recognize that death-thing on the other side of the earth. I've seen them throw it like an arrow for a hundred yards—and I have a notion they're watching that window!"

At sight of the dead wolf and the protruding javelin Celie's face had gone as white as ash. Snatching up one of the pictures from the table, she thrust it into Philip's hand. It was one of the fighting pictures.

"So it's *you?*" he said, smiling at her and trying to keep the tremble of excitement out of his voice. "It's you they want, eh" And they must want you bad. I've never heard of those little devils coming within a hundred miles of this far south. They *must* want you bad. Now—I wonder *why?*" His voice was calm again. It thrilled him to see how utterly she was judging the situation by the movement of his lips and the sound of his voice. With him unafraid she would be unafraid. He judged that quickly. Her eyes bared her faith in him, and suddenly he reached out and took her face between his two hands, and laughed softly, while each instant he feared the smash of a javelin through the window. "I like to see that look in your eyes," he went on. "And I'm almost glad you can't understand me, for I couldn't lie to you worth a cent. I understand those pictures now—and I think we're in a hell of a fix. The Eskimos have followed you and Bram down from the north, and I'm laying a wager with myself that Bram won't return from the caribou hunt. If they were Nunatalmutes or any other tribe I wouldn't be so sure. But they're Kogmollocks. They're worse than the little brown head-hunters of the Philippines when it comes to ambush, and if Bram hasn't got a spear through him this minute I'll never guess again!"

He withdrew his hands from her face, still smiling at her as he talked. The color was returning into her face. Suddenly she made a movement as if to approach the window. He detained her, and in the same moment there came a fierce and snarling outcry from the wolves in the corral. Making Celie understand that she was to remain where he almost forcibly placed her near the table, Philip went again to the window. The pack had gathered close to the gate and two or three of the wolves were leaping excitedly against the sapling bars of their prison. Between the cabin and the gate a second body lay in the snow. Philip's mind leapt to a swift conclusion. The Eskimos had ambushed Bram, and they believed that only the girl was in the cabin. Intuitively he guessed how the superstitious little brown men of the north feared the madman's wolves. One by one they were picking them off with their javelins from outside the corral.

As he looked a head and pair of shoulders rose suddenly above the top of the sapling barrier, an arm shot out and he caught the swift gleam of a javelin as it buried itself in the thick of the pack. In a flash the head and shoulders of the javelin-thrower had disappeared, and in that same moment Philip heard a low cry behind him. Celie had returned to the window. She had seen what he had seen, and her breath came suddenly in a swift and sobbing excitement. In amazement he saw that she was no longer pale. A vivid flush had gathered in each of her cheeks and her eyes blazed with a dark fire. One of her hands caught his arm and her fingers pinched his flesh. He stared dumbly for a moment at the strange transformation in her. He almost believed that she wanted to fight—that she was ready to rush out shoulder to shoulder with him against their enemies. Scarcely had the cry fallen from her lips when she turned and ran swiftly into her room. It seemed to Philip that she was not gone ten seconds. When she returned she thrust into his hand a revolver.

It was a toy affair. The weight and size of the weapon told him that before he broke it and looked at the caliber. It was a "stocking" gun as they called those things in the service, fully loaded with .22 caliber shots and good for a possible partridge at fifteen or twenty paces. Under other conditions it would have furnished him with considerable amusement. But the present was not yesterday or the day before. It was a moment of grim necessity—and the tiny weapon gave him the satisfaction of knowing that he was not entirely helpless against the javelins. It would shoot as far as the stockade, and it might topple a man over if he hit him just right. Anyway, it would make a noise.

A *noise!* The grin that had come into his face died out suddenly as he looked at Celie. He wondered if to her had come the thought that now flashed upon him—if it was that thought that had made her place the revolver in his hand. The blaze of excitement in her wonderful eyes almost told him that it was. With Bram gone, the Eskimos believed she was alone and at their mercy as soon as the wolves were out of the way. Two or three shots from the revolver—and Philip's appearance in the corral—would shake their confidence. It would at least warn them that Celie was not alone, and that her protector was armed. For that reason Philip thanked the Lord that a "stocking" gun had a bark like the explosion of a toy cannon even if its bite was like that of an insect.

David M. Hartford's Production. *A First National Attraction.*

RUTH RENICK IN THE PHOTOPLAY "THE GOLDEN SNARE"

Cautiously he took another look at Bram's wolves. The last javelin had transfixed another of their number and the animal was dragging itself toward the center of the corral. The remaining seven were a dozen yards on the other side of the gate now, leaping and snarling at the stockade, and he knew that the next attack would come from there. He sprang to the door. Celie was only a step behind him as he ran out, and was close at his side when he peered around the end of the cabin.

"They must not see you," he made her understand. "It won't do any good and when they see another man they may possibly get the idea in their heads that you're not here. There can't be many of them or they'd make quicker work of the wolves. I should say not more than—"

"*Se! Se!*"

The warning came in a low cry from Celie's lips. A dark head was appearing slowly above the top of the stockade, and Philip darted suddenly out into the open. The Eskimo did not see him, and Philip waited until he was on the point of hurling his javelin before he made a sound. Then he gave a roar that almost split his throat. In the same instant he began firing. The crack of his pistol and the ferocious outcry he made sent the Eskimo off the stockade like a ball hit by a club. The pack, maddened by their inability to reach their enemies, turned like a flash. Warned by one experience, Philip hustled Celie into the cabin. They were scarcely over the threshold when the wolves were at the door.

"We're sure up against a nice bunch," he laughed, standing for a moment with his arm still about Celie's waist. "A regular *hell* of a bunch, little girl! Now if those wolves only had sense enough to know that we're a little brother and sister to Bram we'd be able to put up a fight that would be some circus. Did you see that fellow topple off the fence? Don't believe I hit him. At least I hope I didn't. If they ever find out the size of this pea-shooter's sting they'll sit up there like a row of crows and laugh at us. But—what a bully *noise* it made!"

He was blissfully unmindful of danger as he held her in the crook of his arm, looking straight into her lovely face as he talked. It was a moment of splendid hypocrisy. He knew that in her excitement and the tremendous effort she was making to understand something of what he was saying that she was unconscious of his embrace. That, and the joyous thrill of the situation, sent the hot blood into his face.

"I'm dangerously near to going the limit," he told her, speaking with a seriousness that would impress her. "I'd fight twenty of those little devils single-handed to know just how you'd take it, and I'd fight another dozen to know who that fellow is in the picture. I'm tempted right now to hug you up close, and kiss you, and let you know how I feel. I'd like to do that—before—anything happens. But would you understand? That's it—would you understand that I love every inch of you from the ground up or would you think I was just beast? That's what I'm afraid of. But I'd like to let you know before I have to put up the big fight for you. And it's coming—if they've got Bram. They'll break down the gate to-night, or burn it, and with the wolves out of the way they'll rush the cabin. And then—"

Slowly he drew his arm from her, and something of the reaction of his thoughts must have betrayed itself in the look that came into his face.

"I guess I've already pulled off a rotten deal on the other fellow," he said, turning to the window. "That is, if you belong to him. And if you didn't why would you stand there with your arms about his neck and he hugging you up like that?"

A few minutes before he had crumpled the picture in his hand and dropped it on the floor. He picked it up now and mechanically smoothed it out as he made his observation through the window. The pack had returned to the stockade. By the aimless manner in which they had scattered he concluded that for the time at least their mysterious enemies had drawn away from the corral.

Celie had not moved. She was watching him earnestly. It seemed to him, as he went to her with the picture, that a new and anxious questioning had come into her eyes. It was as if she had discovered something in him which she had not observed before, something which she was trying to analyze even as he approached her. He felt for the fist time a sense of embarrassment. Was it possible that she had comprehended some word or thought of what he had expressed to her? He could not believe it.

And yet, a woman's intuition—

He held out the picture. Celie took it and for a space looked at it steadily without raising her eyes to meet his. When she did look at him the blue in her eyes was so wonderful and deep and the soul that looked out of them was so clear to his own vision that the shame of that moment's hypocrisy when he had stood with his arm about her submerged him completely. If she had not understood him she at least had guessed.

"*Min fader,*" she said quietly, with the tip of her little forefinger on the man in the picture. "*Min fader.*"

For a moment he thought she had spoken in English.

"Your—your father?" he cried.

She nodded.

"Oo-ee—min fader!"

"Thank the Lord," gasped Philip. And then he suddenly added, "Celie, have you any more cartridges for this popgun? I feel like licking the world!"

CHAPTER XIV

HE tried to hide his jubilation as he talked of more cartridges. He forgot Bram, and the Eskimos waiting outside the corral, and the apparent hopelessness of their situation. *Her father!* He wanted to shout, or dance around the cabin with Celie in his arms. But the change that he had seen come over her made him understand that he must keep hold of himself. He dreaded to see another light come into those glorious blue eyes that had looked at him with such a strange and questioning earnestness a few moments before— the fire of suspicion, perhaps eve of fear if he went too far. He realized that he had betrayed his joy when she had said that the man in the picture was her father. She could not have missed that. And he was not sorry. For him there was an unspeakable thrill in the thought that to a woman, no matter under what sun she is born, there is at least an emotion whose understanding needs no words of speech. And as he had talked to her, sublimely confident that she could not understand him, she had read the betrayal in his face. He was sure of it. And so he talked about cartridges. He talked, he told himself afterwards, like an excited imbecile.

There were no more cartridges. Celie made him understand that. All they possessed were the four that remained in the revolver. As a matter of fact this discovery did not disturb him greatly. At close quarters he would prefer a good club to the pop-gun. Such a club, in the event of a rush attack by the Eskimos, was an important necessity, and he began looking about the cabin to see what he could lay his hand on. He thought of the sapling cross-pieces in Bram's bunk against the wall and tore one out. It was four feet in length and as big around as his fist at one end while at the other it tapered down so that he could grip it easily with his hands.

"Now we're ready for them," he said, testing the poise and swing of the club as he stood in the center of the room. "Unless they burn us out they'll never get through that door. I'm promising you that—s'elp me God I am, Celie!"

As she looked at him a flush burned in her cheeks. He was eager to fight—it seemed to her that he was almost hoping for the attack at the door. It made her splendidly unafraid, and suddenly she laughed softly—a nervous, unexpected little laugh which she could not hold back, and he turned quickly to catch the warm glow in her eyes. Something went up into his throat as she stood there looking at him like that. He had never seen any one quite so beautiful. He dropped his club, and held out his hand.

"Let's shake, Celie," he said. "I'm mighty glad you understand—we're pals."

Unhesitatingly she gave him her hand, and in spite of the fact that death lurked outside they smiled into each other's eyes. After that she went into her room. For half an hour Philip did not see her again.

During that half hour he measured up the situation more calmly. He realized that the exigency was tremendously serious, and that until now he had not viewed it with the dispassionate coolness that characterized the service of the uniform he wore. Celie was accountable for that. He confessed the fact to himself, not without a certain pleasurable satisfaction. He had allowed her presence, and his thoughts of her, to fill the adventure completely for him, and as a result they were now facing an appalling danger. If he had followed his own judgement, and had made Bram Johnson a prisoner, as he should have done in his line of duty, matters would have stood differently.

For several minutes after Celie had disappeared into her room he studied the actions of the wolves in the corral. A short time before he had considered a method of ridding himself of Bram's watchful beasts. Now he regarded them as the one greatest protection they possessed. There were seven left. He was confident they would give warning the moment the Eskimos approached the stockade again. But would their enemies return? The fact that only one man had attacked the wolves at a time was almost convincing evidence that they were very few in number—perhaps only a scouting party of three or four. Otherwise, if they had come in force, they would have made short work of the pack. The thought became a positive conviction as he looked through the window. Bram had fallen a victim to a single javelin, and the scouting party of Kogmollocks had attempted to complete their triumph by carrying Celie back with them to the main body. Foiled in this attempt, and with the knowledge that a new and armed enemy opposed them, they were possibly already on their way for reenforcements.

If this were so there could be but one hope—and that was an immediate escape from the cabin. And between the cabin door and the freedom of the forest were Bram's seven wolves!

A feeling of disgust, almost of anger, swept over him as he drew Celie's little revolver from his pocket and held it in the palm of his hand. There were four cartridges left. But what would they avail against that horde of beasts? They would stop them no more than so many pin-pricks. And what even would the club avail? Against two or three he might put up a fight. But against seven—

He cursed Bram under his breath. It was curious that in that same instant the thought flashed upon him that the wolf-man might not have fallen a victim to the Eskimos. Was it not possible that the spying Kogmollocks had seen him go away on the hunt, and had taken advantage of the opportunity to attack the cabin? They had evidently thought their task would be an easy one. What Philip saw through the window set his pulse beating quickly with the belief that this last conjecture was the true one. The world outside was turning dark. The sky was growing thick and low. In half an hour a storm would break. The Eskimos had foreseen that storm. They knew that the trail taken in their flight, after they had possessed themselves of the girl, would very soon be hidden from the eyes of Bram and the keen scent of his wolves. So they had taken the chance—the chance to make Celie their prisoner before Bram returned.

And why, Philip asked himself, did these savage little barbarians of the north want her? The fighting she had pictured for him had not startled him. For a long time the Kogmollocks had been making trouble. In the last year they had killed a dozen white men along the upper coast, including two American explorers and a missionary. Three patrols had been sent to Coronation Gulf and Bathurst Inlet since August. With the first of those patrols, headed by Olaf Anderson, the Swede, he had come within an ace of going himself. A rumor had come down to Churchill just before he left for the Barrens that Olaf's party of five men had been wiped out. It was not difficult to understand why the Eskimos had attacked Celie Armin's father and those who had come ashore with him from the ship. It was merely a question of lust for white men's blood and white men's plunder, and strangers in their country would naturally be regarded as easy victims. The mysterious and inexplicable part of the affair was their pursuit of the girl. In this pursuit the Kogmollocks had come far beyond the southernmost boundary of their hunting grounds. Philip was sufficiently acquainted with the Eskimos to know that in their veins ran very little of the red-blooded passion of the white man. Matehood was more of a necessity imposed by nature than a joy in their existence, and it was impossible for him to believe that even Celie Armin's beauty had roused the desire for possession among them.

His attention turned to the gathering of the storm. The amazing swiftness with which the gray day was turning into the dark gloom of night fascinated him and he almost called to Celie that she might look upon the phenomenon with him. It was piling in from the vast Barrens to the north and east and for a time it was accompanied by a stillness that was oppressive. He could no longer distinguish a movement in the tops of the cedars and banskian pine beyond the corral. In the corral itself he caught now and then the shadowy, flitting movement of the wolves. He did not hear Celie when she came out of her room. So intently was he straining his eyes to penetrate the thickening pall of gloom that he was unconscious of her presence until she stood close at his side. There was something in the awesome darkening of the world that brought them closer in that moment, and without speaking Philip found her hand and held it in his own. They heard then a low whispering sound—a sound that came creeping up out of the end of the world like a living thing; a whisper so vast that, after a little, it seemed to fill the universe, growing louder and louder until it was no longer a whisper but a moaning, shrieking wail. It was appalling as the first blast of it swept over the cabin. No other place in the world is there storm like the storm that sweeps over the Great Barren: no other place in the world where storm is filled with such a moaning, shrieking tumult of voice. It was not new to Philip. He had heard it when it seemed to him that ten thousand little children were crying under the rolling and twisting onrush of the clouds; he had heard it when it seemed to him the darkness was filled with an army of laughing, shrieking madmen—storm out of which rose piercing human shrieks and the sobbing grief of women's voices. It had driven people mad. Through the long dark night of winter, when for five months they caught no glimpse of the sun, even the Eskimos went *keskwao* and destroyed themselves because of the madness that was in that storm.

And now it swept over the cabin, and in Celie's throat there rose a little sob. So swiftly had darkness gathered that Philip could no longer see her, except where her face made a pale shadow in the gloom, but he could feel the tremble of her body against him. Was it only this morning that he had first seen her, he asked himself? Was it not a long, long time ago, and had she not in that time become, flesh and soul, a part of him? He put out his arms. Warm and trembling and unresisting in that thick gloom she lay within them. His soul rose in a wild ecstasy and rode on the wings of the storm. Closer he held her against his breast, and he said:

"Nothing can hurt you, dear. Nothing—nothing—"

It was a simple and meaningless thing to say—that, and only that. And yet he repeated it over and over again, holding her closer and closer until her heart was throbbing against his own.

"Nothing can hurt you. Nothing—nothing—"

He bent his head. Her face was turned up to him, and suddenly he was thrilled by the warm sweet touch of her lips. He kissed her. She did not strain away from him. He felt—in that darkness—the wild fire in her face.

"Nothing can hurt you, nothing—nothing—" he cried almost sobbingly in his happiness.

Suddenly there came a blast of the storm that rocked the cabin like the butt of a battering-ram, and in that same moment there came from just outside the window a shrieking cry such as Philip had never heard in all his life before. And following the cry there rose above the tumult of the storm the howling of Bram Johnson's wolves.

CHAPTER XV

FOR a space Philip thought that the cry must have come from Bram Johnson himself—that the wolf-man had returned in the pit of the storm. Against his breast Celie had apparently ceased to breathe. Both listened for a repetition of the sound, or for a signal at the barred door. It was strange that in that moment the wind should die down until they could hear the throbbing of their own hearts. Celie's was pounding like a little hammer, and all at once he pressed his face down against hers and laughed with sudden and joyous understanding.

"It was only the wind, dear," he said. "I never heard anything like it before—never! It even fooled the wolves. Bless your dear little heart how it frightened you! And it was enough, too. Shall we light some of Bram's candles?"

He held her hand as he groped his way to where he had seen Bram's supply of bear-dips. She held two of the candles while he lighted them and their yellow flare illumined her face while his own was still in shadow. What he saw in its soft glow and the shine of her eyes made him almost take her in his arms again, candles and all. And then she turned with them and went to the table. He continued to light candles until the sputtering glow of half a dozen of them filled the room. It was a wretched wastefulness, but it was also a moment in which he felt himself fighting to get hold of himself properly. And he felt also the desire to be prodigal about something. When he had lighted his sixth candle, and then faced Celie, she was standing near the table looking at him so quietly and so calmly and with such a wonderful faith in her eyes that he thanked God devoutly he had kissed her only once—just that once! It was a thrilling thought to know that she knew he loved her. There was no doubt of it now. And the thought of what he might have done in that darkness and in the moment of her helplessness sickened him. He could look her straight in the eyes now—unashamed and glad. And she was unashamed, even if a little flushed at what had happened. The same thought was in their minds—and he knew that she was not sorry. Her eyes and the quivering tremble of a smile on her lips told him that. She had braided her hair in that interval when she had gone to her room, and the braid had fallen over her breast and lay there shimmering softly in the candle-glow. He wanted to take her in his arms again. He wanted to kiss her on the mouth and eyes. But instead of that he took the silken braid gently in his two hands and crushed it against his lips.

"I love you," he cried softly. "I love you."

He stood for a moment or two with his head bowed, the thrill of her hair against his face. It was as if he was receiving some kind of a wonderful benediction. And then in a voice that trembled a little she spoke to him. Before he could see fully what was in her eyes she turned suddenly to the wall, took down his coat, and hung it over the window. When he saw her face again it was gloriously flushed. She pointed to the candles.

"No danger of that," he said, comprehending her. "They won't throw any javelins in the storm. Listen!"

It was the wolves again. In a moment their cry was drowned in a crash of the storm that smote the cabin like a huge hand. Again it was wailing over them in a wild orgy of almost human tumult. He could see its swift effect on Celie in spite of her splendid courage. It was not like the surge of mere wind or the roll of thunder. Again he was inspired by the thought of his pocket atlas, and opened it at the large insert map of Canada.

"I'll show you why the wind does that," he explained to her, drawing her to the table and spreading out the map. See, here is the cabin." He made a little black dot with her pencil, and turning to the four walls of Bram's stronghold made her understand what it meant. "And there's the big Barren," he went on tracing it out with the pencil-point. "Up here, you see, is the Arctic ocean, and away over there the Roes Welcome and Hudson's Bay. That's where the storm starts, and when it gets out on the Barren, without a tree or a rock to break its way for five hundred miles—"

He told of the twisting air-currents there and how the storm-clouds sometimes swept so low that they almost smothered one. For a few moments he did not look at Celie or he would have seen something in her face which could not have been because of what he was telling her, and which she could at best only partly understand. She had fixed her eyes on the little black dot. *That* was the cabin. For the first time the map told her where she was, and possibly how she had arrived there. Straight down to that dot from the blue space of the ocean far to the north the map-makers had trailed the course of the Coppermine River. Celie gave an excited little cry and caught Philip's arm, stopping him short in his explanation of the human wailings in the storm. Then she placed a forefinger on the river.

"There—there it is!" she told him, as plainly as though her voice was speaking to him in his own language. "We came down that river. The *Skunnert* landed us *tnere*," and she pointed to the mouth of the Coppermine where it emptied into Coronation Gulf. "And then we came down, down, down—"

He repeated the name of the river.

"The Coppermine."

She nodded, her breath breaking a little in an increasing excitement. She seized the pencil and two-thirds of the distance down the Coppermine made a cross. It was wonderful, he thought, how easily she made him understand. In a low, eager voice she was telling him that where she had put the cross the treacherous Kogmollocks had first attacked them. She described with the pencil their flight away from the river, and after that their return—and a second fight. It was then Bram Johnson had come into the scene. And back there, at the point from which the wolf-man had fled with her, was her father. That was the chief thing she was striving to drive home in his comprehension of the situation. *Her father!* And she believed he was alive, for it was an excitement instead of hopelessness or grief that possessed her as she talked to him. It gave him a sort of shock. He wanted to tell her, with his arms about her, that it was impossible, and that it was his duty to make her realize the truth. Her father was dead now, even if she had last seen him alive. The Kogmollock's had got him, and had undoubtedly hacked him into small pieces, as was their custom when inspired by war-madness. It was inconceivable to think of him as still being alive even if there had been armed friends with him. There was Olaf Anderson and his five men, for instance. Fighters every one of them. And now they were dead. What chance could this other man have?

Her joy when she saw that he understood her added to the uncertainty which was beginning to grip him in spite of all that the day had meant for him. Her faith in him, since that thrilling moment in the darkness, was more than ever like that of a child. She was unafraid of Bram now. She was unafraid of the wolves and the storm and the mysterious pursuers from out of the north. Into his keeping she had placed herself utterly, while this knowledge filled him with a great happiness he was now disturbed by the fact that, if they escaped from the cabin and the Eskimos, she believed he would return with her down the Coppermine in an effort to find her father. He had already made the plans for their escape and they were sufficiently hazardous. Their one chance was to strike south across the thin arm of the Barren for Pierre Breault's cabin. To go in the opposite direction— farther north without dogs or sledge—would be deliberate suicide.

Several times during the afternoon he tried to bring himself to the point of urging on her the naked truth— that her father was dead. There was no doubt of that—not the slightest. But each time he fell a little short. Her confidence in the belief that her father was alive, and that he was where she had marked the cross on the map, puzzled him. Was it conceivable, he asked himself, that the Eskimos had some reason for not killing Paul Armin, and that Celie was aware of the fact? If so he failed to discover it. Again and again he made Celie understand that he wanted to know why the Eskimos wanted her, and each time she answered him with a hopeless little gesture, signifying that she did not know. He did learn that there were two other white men with Paul Armin.

Only by looking at his watch did he know when the night closed in. It was seven o'clock when he led Celie to her room and urged her to go to bed. An hour later, listening at her door, he believed that she was asleep. He had waited for that, and quietly he prepared for the hazardous undertaking he had set for himself. He put on his cap and coat and seized the club he had taken from Bram's bed. Then very cautiously he opened the outer door. A moment later he stood outside, the door closed behind him, with the storm pounding in his face.

Fifty yards away he could not have heard the shout of a man. And yet he listened, gripping his club hard, every nerve in his body strained to a snapping tension. Somewhere within that small circle of the corral were Bram Johnson's wolves, and as he hesitated with his back to the door he prayed that there would come no lull in the storm during the next few minutes. It was possible that he might evade them with the crash and thunder of the gale about him. They could not see him, or hear him, or even smell him in that tumult of wind unless on his way to the gate he ran into them. In that moment he would have given a year of life to have known where they were. Still listening, still fighting to hear some sound of them in the shriek of the storm, he took his first step out into the pit of darkness. He did not run, but went as cautiously as though the night was a dead calm, the club half poised in his hands. He had measured the distance and the direction of the gate and when at last he touched the saplings of the stockade he knew that he could not be far off in his reckoning. Ten paces to the right he found the gate and his heart gave a sudden jump of relief. Half a minute more and it was open. He propped it securely against the beat of the storm with the club he had taken from Bram Johnson's bed.

Then he turned back to the cabin, with the little revolver clutched in his hand, and his face was strained and haggard when he found the door and returned again into the glow of the candlelight. In the center of the room, her face as white as his own, stood Celie. A great fear must have gripped her, for she stood there in her sleeping gown with her hands clutched at her breast, her eyes staring at him in speechless questioning. He explained by opening the door a bit and pantomiming to the gate outside the cabin "The wolves will be gone in the morning," he said, a ring of triumph in his voice. "I have opened the gate. There is nothing in our way now."

  She understood. Her eyes were a glory to look into then. Her fingers unclenched at her breast, she gave a short, quick breath and a little cry—and her arms almost reached out to him. He was afraid of himself as he went to her and led her again to the door of her room. And there for a moment they paused, and she looked up into his face. Her hand crept from his and went softly to his shoulder. She said something to him, almost in a whisper, and he could no longer fight against the pride and the joy and the faith he saw in her eyes. He bent down, slowly so that she might draw away from him if she desired, and kissed her upturned lips. And then, with a strange little cry that was like the soft note of a bird, she turned from him and disappeared into the darkness of her room. A great deal of that night's storm passed over his head unheard after that. It was late when he went to bed. He crowded Bram's long box-stove with wood before he extinguished the last candle. And for an hour after that he lay awake, thinking of Celie and of the great happiness that had come into his life all in one day. During that hour he made the plans of a lifetime. Then he, too, fell into sleep—a restless, uneasy slumber filled with many visions. For a time there had come a lull in the gale, but now it broke over the cabin in increased fury. A hand seemed slapping at the window, threatening to break it, and a volley of wind and snow shot suddenly down the chimney, forcing open the stove door, so that a shaft of ruddy light cut like a red knife through the dense gloom of the cabin. In varying ways the sounds played a part in Philip's dreams. In all those dreams, and segments of dreams, the girl was present. It was strange that in all of them she should be his wife. And it was strange that the big woods and the deep snows played no part in them. He was back home. And Celie was with him. Once they went for wildflowers and were caught in a thunderstorm, and ran to an old and disused barn in the center of a field for shelter. He could feel Celie trembling against him, and he was stroking her hair as the thunder crashed over them and the lightning filled her eyes with fear. After that there came to him a vision of early autumn nights when they went corn-roasting, with other young people. He had always been afflicted with a slight nasal trouble, and smoke irritated him. It set him sneezing, and kept him dodging about the fire, and Celie was laughing as the smoke persisted in following him about, like a young scamp of a boy bent on tormenting him. The smoke was unusually persistent on this particular night, until at last the laughter went out of the girl's face, and she ran into his arms and covered his eyes with her soft hands. Restlessly he tossed in his bunk, and buried his face in the blanket that answered for a pillow. The smoke reached him even there, and he sneezed chokingly. In that instant Celie's face disappeared. He sneezed again—and awoke.

In that moment his dazed senses adjusted themselves. The cabin was full of smoke. It partly blinded him, but through it he could see tongues of fire shooting toward the ceiling. He heard then the crackling of burning pitch—a dull and consuming roar, and with a stifled cry he leaped from his bunk and stood on his feet. Dazed by the smoke and flame, he saw that there was not the hundredth part of a second to lose. Shouting Celie's name he ran to her door, where the fire was already beginning to shut him out. His first cry had awakened her and she was facing the lurid glow of the flame as he rushed in. Almost before she could comprehend what was happening he had wrapped one of the heavy bear skins about her and had swept her into his arms. With her face crushed against his breast he lowered his head and dashed back into the fiery holocaust of the outer room. The cabin, with its pitch-filled logs, was like a box made of tinder, and a score of men could not have beat out the fire that was raging now. The wind beating from the west had kept it from reaching the door opening into the corral, but the pitch was hissing and smoking at the threshold as Philip plunged through the blinding pall and fumbled for the latch.

Not ten seconds too soon did he stagger with his burden out into the night. As the wind drove in through the open door the flames seemed to burst in a sudden explosion and the cabin was a seething snarl of flame. It burst through the window and out of the chimney and Philip's path to the open gate was illumined by a fiery glow. Not until he had passed beyond the stockade to the edge of the forest did he stop and look back. Over their heads the wind wailed and moaned in the spruce tops, but even above that sound came the roar of the fire. Against his breast Philip heard a sobbing cry, and suddenly he held the girl closer, and crushed his face down against hers, fighting to keep back the horror that was gripping at his heart. Even as he felt her arms creeping up out of the bear skin and clinging about his neck he felt upon him like a weight of lead the hopelessness of a despair as black as the night itself. The cabin was now a pillar of flames, and in it was everything that had made life possible for them. Food, shelter, clothing—all were gone. In this moment he did not think of himself, but of the girl he held in his arms, and he strained her closer and kissed her lips and her eyes and her tumbled hair there in the storm-swept darkness, telling her what he knew was now a lie—that she was safe, that nothing could harm her. Against him he felt the tremble and throb of her soft body, and it was this that filled him with the horror of the thing—the terror of the thought that her one garment was a bear skin. He had felt, a moment before, the chill touch of a naked little foot.

And yet he kept saying, with his face against hers:

"It's all right, little sweetheart. We'll come out all right—we sure will!"

CHAPTER XVI

His first impulse, after those few appalling seconds following their escape from the fire, was to save something from the cabin. Still talking to Celie he dropped on his knees and tucked her up warmly in the bear skin, with her back to a tree. He thanked God that it was a big skin and that it enveloped her completely. Leaving her there he ran back through the gate. He no longer feared the wolves. If they had not already escaped into the forest he knew they would not attack him in that hot glare of the one thing above all others they feared—fire. For a space, thought of the Eskimos, and the probability of the fire bringing them from wherever they had sought shelter from the storm, was secondary to the alarming necessity which faced him. Because of his restlessness and his desire to be ready for any emergency he had not undressed when he threw himself on his bunk that night, but he was without a coat or cap. And Celie! He cried out aloud in his anguish when he stopped just outside the deadline of the furnace of flame that was once the cabin, and standing there with clenched hands he cursed himself for the carelessness that had brought her face to face with a peril deadlier than the menace of the Eskimos or Bram Johnson's wolves. He alone was responsible. His indiscretion in overfilling the stove had caused the fire, and in that other moment—when he might have snatched up more than the bear skin—his mind had failed to act.

In the short space he stood there helplessly in the red heat of the fire the desperateness of the situation seared itself like the hot flame itself in his brain. As prisoners in Bram's cabin, guarded by the wolves and attacked by the Eskimos, they still had shelter, food, clothing—a chance to live, at least the chance to fight. And now—

He put a hand to his bare head and faced the direction of the storm. With the dying away of the wind snow had begun to fall, and with this snow he knew there would come a rising temperature. It was probably twenty degrees below zero, and unless the wind went down completely his ears would freeze in an hour or two. Then he thought of the thick German socks he wore. One of them would do for a cap. His mind worked swiftly after that. There was, after all, a tremendous thrill in the thought of fighting the odds against him, and in the thought of the girl waiting for him in the bear skin, her life depending upon him utterly now. Without him she could not move from the tree where he had left her unless her naked feet buried themselves in the snow. If something happened to him—she would die. Her helplessness filled him suddenly with a wild exultation, the joy of absolute possession that leapt for an instant or two above his fears. She was something more—now—than the woman he loved. She was a little child, to be carried in his arms, to be sheltered from the wind and the cold until the last drop of blood had ceased to flow in his veins. His was the mighty privilege now to mother her until the end came for them both— or some miracle saved them. The last barrier was gone from between them. That he had met her only yesterday was an unimportant incident now. The world had changed, life had changed, a long time had passed. She belonged to him as utterly as the stars belonged to the skies. In his arms she would find life—or death. He was braced for the fight. His mind, riding over its first fears, began to shape itself for action even as he turned back toward the edge of the forest. Until then he had not thought of the other cabin— the cabin which Bram and he had passed on their way in from the Barren. His heart rose up suddenly in his throat and he wanted to shout. That cabin was their salvation! It was not more than eight or ten miles away, and he was positive that he could find it.

He ran swiftly through the increasing circle of light made by the burning logs. If the Eskimos had not gone far some one of them would surely see the red glow of the fire, and discovery now meant death. In the edge of the trees, where the shadows were deep, he paused and looked back. His hand fumbled where the left-pocket of his coat would have been, and as he listened to the crackling of the flames and stared into the heart of the red glow there smote him with sudden and sickening force a realization of their deadliest peril. In that twisting inferno of burning pitch was his coat, and in the left-hand pocket of that coat *were his matches!*

Fire! Out there in the open a seething, twisting mass of it, taunting him with its power, mocking him as pitiless as the mirage mocks a thirst-crazed creature of the desert. In an hour or two it would be gone. He might keep up its embers for a time—until the Eskimos, or starvation, or still greater storm put an end to it. The effort, in any event, would be futile in the end. Their one chance lay in finding the other cabin, and reaching it quickly. When it came to the point of absolute necessity he could at least try to make fire as he had seen an Indian make it once, though at the time he had regarded the achievement as a miracle born of unnumbered generations of practice.

He heard the glad note of welcome in Celie's throat when he returned to her. She spoke his name. It seemed to him that there was no note of fear in her voice, but just gladness that he had come back to her in that pit of darkness. He bent down and tucked her snugly in the big bear skin before he took her up in his arms again. He held her so that her face was snuggled close against his neck, and he kissed her soft mouth again, and whispered to her as he began picking his way through the forest. His voice, whispering, made her understand that they must make no sound. She was tightly imprisoned in the skin, but all at once he felt one of her hands work its way out of the warmth of it and lay against his cheek. It did not move away from his face. Out of her soul and body there passed through that contact of her hand the confession that made him equal to fighting the world. For many minutes after that neither of them spoke. The moan of the wind was growing less and less in the treetops, and once Philip saw a pale break where the clouds had split asunder in the sky. The storm was at an end—and it was almost dawn. In a quarter of an hour the shotlike snow of the blizzard had changed to big soft flakes that dropped straight out of the clouds in a white deluge. By the time day came their trail would be completely hidden from the eyes of the Eskimos.

Because of that Philip traveled as swiftly as the darkness and the roughness of the forest would allow him. As nearly as he could judge he kept due east. For a considerable time he did not feel the weight of the precious burden in his arms. He believed that they were at least half a mile from the burned cabin before he paused to rest. Even then he spoke to Celie in a low voice. He had stopped where the trunk of a fallen tree lay as high as his waist, and on this he seated the girl, holding her there in the crook of his arm. With his other hand he fumbled to see if the bear skin protected her fully, and in the investigation his hand came in contact again with one of her bare feet. Celie gave a little jump. Then she laughed, and he made sure that the foot was snug and warm before he went on.

Twice in the next half mile he stopped. The third time, a full mile from the cabin, was in a dense growth of spruce through the tops of which snow and wind did not penetrate. Here he made a nest of spruce-boughs for Celie, and they waited for the day. In the black interval that precedes Arctic dawn they listened for sounds that might come to them. Just once came the wailing howl of one of Bram's wolves, and twice Philip fancied that he heard the distant cry of a human voice. The second time Celie's fingers tightened about his own to tell him that she, too, had heard.

A little later, leaving Celie alone, Philip went back to the edge of the spruce thicket and examined closely their trail where it had crossed a bit of open. It was not half an hour old, yet the deluge of snow had almost obliterated the signs of their passing. His one hope was that the snowfall would continue for another hour. By that time there would not be a visible track of man or beast, except in the heart of the thickets. But he knew that he was not dealing with white men or Indians now. The Eskimos were night-trackers and night-hunters. For five months out of every twelve their existence depended upon their ability to stalk and kill in darkness. If they had returned to the burning cabin it was possible, even probable, that they were close on their heels now.

For a second time he found himself a stout club. He waited, listening, and straining his eyes to penetrate the thick gloom; and then, as his own heart-beats came to him audibly, he felt creeping over him a slow and irresistible foreboding—a premonition of something impending, of a great danger close at hand. His muscles grew tense, and he clutched the club, ready for action.

CHAPTER XVII

IT seemed to Philip, as he stood with the club ready in his hand, that the world had ceased to breathe in its anticipation of the thing for which he was waiting—and listening. The wind had dropped dead. There was not a rustle in the tree-tops, not a sound to break the stillness. The silence, so close after storm, was an Arctic phenomenon which did not astonish him, and yet the effect of it was almost painfully gripping. Minor sounds began to impress themselves on his senses—the soft murmur of the falling snow, his own breath, the pounding of his heart. He tried to throw off the strange feeling that oppressed him, but it was impossible. Out there in the darkness he would have sworn that there were eyes and ears strained as his own were strained. And the darkness was lifting. Shadows began to disentangle themselves from the gray chaos. Trees and bushes took form, and over his head the last heavy windrows of clouds shouldered their way out of the sky.

Still, as the twilight of dawn took the place of night, he did not move, except to draw himself a little closer into the shelter of the scrub spruce behind which he had hidden himself. He wondered if Celie would be frightened at his absence. But he could not compel himself to go on—or back. *Something was coming!* He was as positive of it as he was of the fact that night was giving place to day. Yet he could see nothing—hear nothing. It was light enough now for him to see movement fifty yards away, and he kept his eyes fastened on the little open across which their trail had come. If Olaf Anderson the Swede had been there he might have told him of another night like this, and another vigil. For Olaf had learned that the Eskimos, like the wolves, trail two by two and four by four, and that—again like the wolves—they pursue not *on* the trail but with the trail between them.

But it was the trail that Philip watched; and as he kept his vigil—that inexplicable mental undercurrent telling him that his enemies were coming—his mind went back sharply to the girl a hundred yards behind him. The acuteness of the situation sent question after question rushing through his mind, even as he gripped his club. For her he was about to fight. For her he was ready to kill, and not afraid to die. He loved her. And yet—she was a mystery. He had held her in his arms, had felt her heart beating against his breast, had kissed her lips and her eyes and her hair, and her response had been to place herself utterly within the shelter of his arms. She had given herself to him and he was possessed of the strength of one about to fight for his own. And with that strength the questions pounded again in his head. *Who was she? And for what reason were mysterious enemies coming after her through the gray dawn?*

In that moment he heard a sound. His heart stood suddenly still. He held his breath. It was a sound almost indistinguishable from the whisper of the air and the trees and yet it smote upon his senses like the detonation of a thunder-clap. It was more of a *presence* than a sound. The trail was clear. He could see to the far side of the open now, and there was no movement. He turned his head—slowly and without movement of his body, and in that instant a gasp rose to his lips, and died there. Scarcely a dozen paces from him stood a poised and hooded figure, a squat, fire-eyed apparition that looked more like monster than man in that first glance. Something acted within him that was swifter than reason—a sub-conscious instinct that works for self-preservation like the flash of powder in a pan. It was this sub-conscious self that received the first photographic impression—the strange poise of the hooded creature, the uplifted arm, the cold, streaky gleam of something in the dawn-light, and in response to that impression Philip's physical self crumpled down in the snow as a javelin hissed through the space where his head and shoulders had been.

So infinitesimal was the space of time between the throwing of the javelin and Philip's movement that the Eskimo believed he had transfixed his victim. A scream of triumph rose in his throat. It was the Kogmollock *sakootwow*—the blood-cry, a single shriek that split the air for a mile. It died in another sort of cry. From where he had dropped Philip was up like a shot. His club swung through the air and before the amazed hooded creature could dart either to one side or the other it had fallen with crushing force. That one blow must have smashed his shoulder to a pulp. As the body lurched downward another blow caught the hooded head squarely and the beginning of a second cry ended in a sickening grunt. The force of the blow carried Philip half off his feet, and before he could recover himself two other figures had rushed upon him from out of the gloom. Their cries as they came at him were like the cries of beasts. Philip had no time to use his club. From his unbalanced position he flung himself upward and at the nearest of his enemies, saving himself from the upraised javelin by clinching. His fist shot out and caught the Eskimo squarely in the mouth. He struck again—and the javelin dropped from the Kogmollock's hand. In that moment, every vein in his body pounding with the rage and excitement of battle, Philip let out a yell. The end of it was stifled by a pair of furry arms. His head snapped back—and he was down.

A thrill of horror shot through him. It was the one unconquerable fighting trick of the Eskimos—that neck hold. Caught from behind there was no escape from it. It was the age-old *sasaki-wechikun*, or sacrifice-hold, an inheritance that came down from father to son—the Arctic jiu-jitsu by which one Kogmollock holds the victim helpless while a second cuts out his heart. Flat on his back, with his head and shoulders bent under him, Philip lay still for a single instant. He heard the shrill command of the Eskimo over him—an exhortation for the other to hurry up with the knife. And then, even as he heard a grunting reply, his hand came in contact with the pocket which held Celie's little revolver. He drew it quickly, cocked it under his back, and twisting his arm until the elbow-joint cracked, he fired. It was a chance shot. The powder-flash burned the murderous, thick lipped face in the sealskin hood. There was no cry, no sound that Philip heard. But the arms relaxed about his neck. He rolled over and sprang to his feet. Three or four paces from him was the Eskimo he had struck, crawling toward him on his hands and knees, still dazed by the blows he had received. In the snow Philip saw his club. He picked it up and replaced the revolver in his pocket. A single blow as the groggy Eskimo staggered to his feet and the fight was over.

It had taken perhaps three or four minutes—no longer than that. His enemies lay in three dark and motionless heaps in the snow. Fate had played a strong hand with him. Almost by a miracle he had escaped and at least two of the Eskimos were dead.

He was still watchful, still guarding against a further attack, and suddenly he whirled to face a figure that brought from him a cry of astonishment and alarm. It was Celie. She was standing ten paces from him, and in the wild terror that had brought her to him she had left the bear skin behind. Her naked feet were buried in the snow. Her arms, partly bared, were reaching out to him in the gray Arctic dawn, and then wildly and moaningly there came to him——

"Philip—Philip—"

He sprang to her, a choking cry on his own lips. This, after all, was the last proof—when she had thought that their enemies were killing him *she had come to him*. He was sobbing her name like a boy as he ran back with her in his arms. Almost fiercely he wrapped the bear skin about her again, and then crushed her so closely in his arms that he could hear her gasping faintly for breath. In that wild and glorious moment he listened. A cold and leaden day was breaking over the world and as they listened their hearts throbbing against each other, the same sound came to them both.

It was the *sakootwow*—the savage, shrieking blood-cry of the Kogmollocks, a scream that demanded an answer of the three hooded creatures who, a few minutes before, had attacked Philip in the edge of the open. The cry came from perhaps a mile away. And then faintly, it was answered far to the west. For a moment Philip pressed his face down to Celie's In his heart was a prayer, for he knew that the fight had only begun.

CHAPTER XVIII

THAT the Eskimos both to the east and the west were more than likely to come their way, converging toward the central cry that was now silent, Philip was sure. In the brief interval in which he had to act he determined to make use of his fallen enemies. This he impressed on Celie's alert mind before he ran back to the scene of the fight. He made no more than a swift observation of the field in these first moments—did not even look for weapons. His thought was entirely of Celie. The smallest of the three forms on the snow was the Kogmollock he had struck down with his club. He dropped on his knees and took off first the sealskin *bashlyk*, or hood. Then he began stripping the dead man of his other garments. From the fur coat to the caribou-skin moccasins they were comparatively new. With them in his arms he hurried back to the girl.

It was not a time for fine distinctions. The clothes were a godsend, though they had come from a dead man's back. Celie's eyes shone with joy. It amazed him more than ever to see how unafraid she was in this hour of great danger. She was busy with the clothes almost before his back was turned.

He returned to the Eskimos. The three were dead. It made him shudder—one with a tiny bullet hole squarely between the eyes and the others crushed by the blows of the club. His hand fondled Celie's little revolver—the peashooter he had laughed at. After all it had saved his life. And the club—

He did not examine too closely there. From the man he had struck with his naked fist he outfitted himself with a hood and *temiak*, or coat. In the *temiak* there were no pockets, but at the waist of each of the dead men was a narwhal skin pouch which answered for all pockets. He tossed the three pouches in a little heap on the snow before he searched for weapons. He found two knives and half a dozen of the murderous little javelins. One of the knives was still clutched in the hand of the Eskimo who was creeping up to disembowel him when Celie's revolver saved him. He took this knife because it was longer and sharper than the other.

On his knees he began to examine the contents of the three pouches. In each was the inevitable roll of *babiche*, or caribou-skin cord, and a second and smaller waterproof narwhal bag in which were the Kogmollock fire materials. There was no food. This fact was evident proof that the Eskimos were in camp somewhere in the vicinity. He had finished his investigation of the pouches when, looking up from his kneeling posture, he saw Celie approaching.

In spite of the grimness of the situation he could not repress a smile as he rose to greet her. At fifty paces, even with her face toward him, one would easily make the error of mistaking her for an Eskimo, as the sealskin *bashlyk* was so large that it almost entirely concealed her face except when one was very close to her. Philip's first assistance was to roll back the front of the hood. Then he pulled her thick braid out from under the coat and loosed the shining glory of her hair until it enveloped her in a wonderful shimmering mantle. Their enemies could not mistake her for a man now, even at a hundred yards. If they ran into an ambuscade she would at least be saved from the javelins.

Celie scarcely realized what he was doing. She was staring at the dead men—silent proof of the deadly menace that had threatened them and of the terrific fight Philip must have made. A strange note rose in her throat, and turning toward him suddenly she flung herself into his arms. Her own arms encircled his neck, and for a space she lay shudderingly against his breast, as if sobbing. How many times he kissed her in those moments Philip could not have told. It must have been a great many. He knew only that her arms were clinging tighter and tighter about his neck, and that she was whispering his name, and that his hands were buried in her soft hair. He forgot time, forgot the possible cost of precious seconds lost. It was a small thing that recalled him to his senses. From out of a spruce top a handful of snow fell on his shoulder. It startled him like the touch of a strange hand, and in another moment he was explaining swiftly to Celie that there were other enemies near and that they must lose no time in flight.

He fastened one of the pouches at his waist, picked up his club, and—on second thought—one of the Kogmollock javelins. He had no very definite idea of how he might use the latter weapon, as it was too slender to be of much avail as a spear at close quarters. At a dozen paces he might possibly throw it with some degree of accuracy. In a Kogmollock's hand it was a deadly weapon at a hundred paces. With the determination to be at his side when the next fight came Celie possessed herself of a second javelin. With her hand in his Philip set out then due north through the forest.

It was in that direction he knew the cabin must lay. After striking the edge of the timber after crossing the Barren Bram Johnson had turned almost directly south, and as he remembered the last lap of the journey Philip was confident that not more than eight or ten miles had separated the two cabins. He regretted now his carelessness in not watching Bram's trail more closely in that last hour or two. His chief hope of finding the cabin was in the discovery of some landmark at the edge of the Barren. He recalled distinctly where they had turned in to the forest, and in less than half an hour after that they had come upon the first cabin.

Their immediate necessity was not so much the finding of the cabin as escape from the Eskimos. Within half an hour, perhaps even less, he believed that other eyes would know of the fight at the edge of the open. It was inevitable. If the Kogmollocks on either side of them struck the trail before it reached the open they would very soon run upon the dead, and if they came upon footprints in the snow this side of the open they would back-trail swiftly to learn the source and meaning of the cry of triumph that had not repeated itself. Celie's little feet, clad in moccasins twice too big for her, dragged in the snow in a way that would leave no doubt in the Eskimo mind. As Philip saw the situation there was one chance for them, and only one. They could not escape by means of strategy. They could not hide from their pursuers. Hope depended entirely upon the number of their enemies. If there were only three or four of them left they would not attack in the open. In that event he must watch for ambuscade, and dread the night. He looked down at Celie, buried in her furry coat and hood and plodding along courageously at his side with her hand in his. This was not a time in which to question him, and she was obeying his guidance with the faith of a child. It was tremendous, he thought—the most wonderful moment that had ever entered into his life. It is this dependence, this sublime faith and confidence in him of the woman he loves that gives to a man the strength of a giant in the face of a great crisis and makes him put up a tiger's fight for her. For such a woman a man must win. And then Philip noticed how tightly Celie's other hand was gripping the javelin with which she had armed herself. She was ready to fight, too. The thrill of it all made him laugh, and her eyes shot up to him suddenly, filled with a moment's wonder that he should be laughing now. She must have understood, for the big hood hid her face again almost instantly, and her fingers tightened the smallest bit about his.

For a matter of a quarter of an hour they traveled as swiftly as Celie could walk. Philip was confident that the Eskimo whose cries they had heard would strike directly for the point whence the first cry had come, and it was his purpose to cover as much distance as possible in the first few minutes that their enemies might be behind them. It was easier to watch the back trail than to guard against ambuscades ahead. Twice in that time he stopped where they would be unseen and looked back, and in advancing he picked out the thinnest timber and evaded whatever might have afforded a hiding place to a javelin-thrower. They had progressed another half mile when suddenly they came upon a snowshoe trail in the snow.

It had crossed at right angles to their own course, and as Philip bent over it a sudden lump rose into his throat. The other Eskimos had not worn snowshoes. That in itself had not suprised him, for the snow was hard and easily traveled in moccasins. The fact that amazed him now was that the trail under his eyes had not been made by Eskimo *usamuks*. The tracks were long and narrow. The web imprint in the snow was not that of the broad narwhal strip, but the finer mesh of *babiche*. It was possible that an Eskimo was wearing them, but they were *a white man's shoes!*

And then he made another discovery. For a dozen paces he followed in the trail, allowing six inches with each step he took as the snowshoe handicap. Even at that he could not easily cover the tracks. The man who had made them had taken a longer snowshoe stride than his own by at least nine inches. He could no longer keep the excitement of his discovery from Celie. "The Eskimo never lived who could make that track," he exclaimed. "They can travel fast enough but they're a bunch of runts when it comes to leg-swing. It's a white man—or Bram!"

The announcement of the wolf-man's name and Philip's gesture toward the trail drew a quick little cry of understanding from Celie. In a flash she had darted to the snowshoe tracks and was examining them with eager intensity. Then she looked up and shook her head. It wasn't Bram! She pointed to the tail of the shoe and catching up a twig broke it under Philip's eyes. He remembered now. The end of Bram's shoes was snubbed short off. There was no evidence of that defect in the snow. It was not Bram who had passed that way.

For a space he stood undecided. He knew that Celie was watching him—that she was trying to learn something of the tremendous significance of that moment from his face. The same unseen force that had compelled him to wait and watch for his foes a short time before seemed urging him now to follow the strange snowshoe trail. Enemy or friend the maker of those tracks would at least be armed. The thought of what a rifle and a few cartridges would mean to him and Celie now brought a low cry of decision from him. He turned quickly to Celie.

"He's going east—and we ought to go north to find the cabin," he told her, pointing to the trail. "But we'll follow him. I want his rifle. I want it more than anything else in this world, now that I've got you. We'll follow—"

If there had been a shadow of hesitation in his mind it was ended in that moment. From behind them there came a strange hooting cry. It was not a yell such as they had heard before. It was a booming far-reaching note that had in it the intonation of a drum—a sound that made one shiver because of its very strangeness. And then, from farther west, it came—

"*Hoom—Hoom—Ho-o-o-o-o-m-m-m-m—*"

In the next half minute it seemed to Philip that the cry was answered from half a dozen different quarters. Then again it came from directly behind them.

Celie uttered a little gasp as she clung to his hand again. She understood as well as he. One of the Eskimos had discovered the dead and their foes were gathering in behind them.

CHAPTER XIX

BEFORE the last of the cries had died away Philip flung far to one side of the trail the javelin he carried, and followed it up with Celie's, impressing on her that every ounce of additional weight meant a handicap for them now. After the javelins went his club.

"It's going to be the biggest race I've ever run," he smiled at her. "And we've got to win. If we don't—"

Celie's eyes were aglow as she looked at him. He was splendidly calm. There was no longer a trace of excitement in his face, and he was smiling at her even as he picked her up suddenly in his arms. The movement was so unexpected that she gave a little gasp. Then she found herself borne swiftly over the trail. For a distance of a hundred yards Philip ran with her before he placed her on her feet again. In no better way could he have impressed on her that they were partners in a race against death and that every energy must be expended in that race. Scarecely had her feet touched the snow than she was running at his side, her hand clasped in his. Barely a second was lost.

With the swift directness of the trained man-hunter Philip had measured his chances of winning. The Eskimos, first of all, would gather about their dead. After one or two formalities they would join in a chattering council, all of which meant precious time for them. The pursuit would be more or less cautious because of the bullet hole in the Kogmollock's forehead.

If it had been possible for Celie to ask him just what he expected to gain by following the strange snowshoe trail he would have had difficulty in answering. It was, like his single shot with Celie's little revolver, a chance gamble against big odds. A number of possibilities had suggested themselves to him. It even occurred to him that the man who was hurrying toward the east might be a member of the Royal Northwest Mounted Police. Of one thing, however, he was confident. The maker of the tracks would not be armed with javelins. He would have a rifle. Friend or foe, he was after that rifle. The trick was to catch sight of him at the earliest possible moment.

How much of a lead the stranger had was a matter at which he could guess with considerable accuracy. The freshness of the trail was only slightly dimmed by snow, which was ample proof that it had been made at the very tail-end of the storm. He believed that it was not more than an hour old.

For a good two hundred yards Philip set a dog-trot pace for Celie, who ran courageously at his side. At the end of that distance he stopped. Celie was panting for breath. Her hood had slipped back and her face was flushed like a wild-flower by her exertion. Her eyes shone like stars, and her lips were parted a little. She was temptingly lovely, but again Philip lost not a second of unnecessary time. He picked her up in his arms again and continued the race. By using every ounce of his own strength and endurance in this way he figured that their progress would be at least a third faster than the Eskimos who would follow. The important question was how long he could keep up the pace.

Against his breast Celie was beginning to understand his scheme as plainly as if he had explained it to her in words. At the end of the fourth hundred yards she let him know that she was ready to run another lap. He carried her on fifty yards more before he placed her on her feet. In this way they had gone three-quarters of a mile when the trail turned abruptly from its easterly course to a point of the compass due north. So sharp was the turn that Philip paused to investigate the sudden change in direction. The stranger had evidently stood for several minutes at this point, which was close to the blasted stub of a dead spruce. In the snow Philip observed for the first time a number of dark brown spots.

"Here is where he took a new bearing—and a chew of tobacco," said Philip, more to himself than to Celie. "And there's no snow in his tracks. By George, I don't believe he's got more than half an hour's start of us this minute!" It was his turn to carry Celie again, and in spite of her protest that she was still good for another run he resumed their pursuit of the stranger with her in his arms. By her quick breathing and the bit of tenseness that had gathered about her mouth he knew that the exertion she had already been put to was having its effect on her. For her little feet and slender body the big moccasins and cumbersome fur garments she wore were a burden in themselves, even at a walk. He found that by holding her higher in his arms, with her own arms encircling his shoulders, it was easier to run with her at the pace he had set for himself. And when he held her in this way her hair covered his breast and shoulders so that now and then his face was smothered in the velvety sweetness of it. The caress of it and the thrill of her arms about him spurred him on. Once he made three hundred yards. But he was gulping for breath when he stopped. That time Celie compelled him to let her run a little farther, and when they paused she was swaying on her feet, and panting. He carried her only a hundred and fifty yards in the interval after that. Both realized what it meant. The pace was telling on them. The strain of it was in Celie's eyes. The flower-like flush of her first exertion was gone from her face. It was pale and a little haggard, and in Philip's face she saw the beginning of the thing which she did not realize was betraying itself so plainly in her own. She put her hands up to his cheeks, and smiled. It was tremendous—that moment—her courage, her splendid pride in him, her manner of telling him that she was not afraid as her little hands lay against his face. For the first time he gave way to his desire to hold her close to him, and kiss the sweet mouth she held up to his as her head nestled on his breast.

After a moment or two he looked at his watch. Since striking the strange trail they had traveled forty minutes. In that time they had covered at least three miles, and were a good four miles from the scene of the fight. It was a big start. The Eskimos were undoubtedly a half that distance behind them, and the stranger whom they were following could not be far ahead.

They went on at a walk. For the third time they came to a point in the trail where the stranger had stopped to make observations. It was apparent to Philip that the man he was after was not quite sure of himself. Yet he did not hesitate in the course due north.

For half an hour they continued in that direction. Not for an instant now did Philip allow his caution to lag. Eyes and ears were alert for sound or movement either behind or ahead of them, and more and more frequently he turned to scan the back trail.

They were at least five miles from the edge of the open where the fight had occurred when they came to the foot of a ridge, and Philip's heart gave a sudden thump of hope. He remembered that ridge. It was a curiously formed "hogback"—like a great windrow of snow piled up and frozen. Probably it was miles in length. Somewhere he and Bram had crossed it soon after passing the first cabin. He had not tried to tell Celie of this cabin. Time had been too precious. But now, in the short interval of rest he allowed themselves, he drew a picture of it in the snow and made her understand that it was somewhere close to the ridge and that it looked as though the stranger was making for it. He half carried Celie up the ridge after that. She could not hide from him that her feet were dragging even at a walk. Exhaustion showed in her face, and once when she tried to speak to him her voice broke in a little gasping sob. On the far side of the ridge he took her in his arms and carried her again.

"It can't be much farther," he encouraged her. "We've got to overtake him pretty soon, dear. Mighty soon." Her hand pressed gently against his cheek, and he swallowed a thickness that in spite of his effort gathered in his throat. During that last half hour a different look had come into her eyes. It was there now as she lay limply with her head on his breast—a look of unutterable tenderness, and of something else. It was that which brought the thickness into his throat. It was not fear. It was the soft glow of a great love—and of understanding. She knew that even he was almost at the end of his fight. His endurance was giving out. One of two things must happen very soon. She continued to stroke his cheek gently until he placed her on her feet again, and then she held one of his hands close to her breast as they looked behind them, and listened. He could feel the soft throbbing of her heart. If he needed greater courage then it was given to him.

They went on. And then, so suddenly that it brought a stifled cry from the girl's lips, they came upon the cabin. It was not a hundred yards from them when they first saw it. It was no longer abandoned. A thin spiral of smoke was rising from the chimney. There was no sign of life other than that.

For half a minute Philip stared at it. Here, at last, was the final hope. Life or death, all that the world might hold for him and the girl at his side, was in that cabin. Gently he drew her so that she would be unseen. And then, still looking at the cabin, he drew off his coat and dropped it in the snow. It was the preparation of a man about to fight. The look of it was in his face and the stiffening of his muscles, and when he turned to his little companion she was as white as the snow under her feet.

"We're in time," he breathed. "You—you stay here."

She understood. Her hands clutched at him as he left her. A gulp rose in her throat. She wanted to call out. She wanted to hold him back—or go with him. Yet she obeyed. She stood with a heart that choked her and watched him go. For she knew, after all, that it was the thing to do. Sobbingly she breathed his name. It was a prayer. For she knew what would happen in the cabin.

CHAPTER XX

PHILIP came up behind the windowless end of the cabin. He noticed in passing with Bram that on the opposite side was a trap-window of saplings, and toward this he moved swiftly but with caution. It was still closed when he came where he could see. But with his ear close to the chinks he heard a sound—the movement of some one inside. For an instant he looked over his shoulder. Celie was standing where he had left her. He could almost feel the terrible suspense that was in her eyes as she watched him.

He moved around toward the door. There was in him an intense desire to have it over with quickly. His pulse quickened as the thought grew in him that the maker of the strange snowshoe trail might be a friend after all. But how was he to discover that fact? He had decided to take no chances in the matter. Ten seconds of misplaced faith in the stranger might prove fatal. Once he held a gun in his hands he would be in a position to wait for introductions and explanations. But until then, with their Eskimo enemies close at their heels—

His mind did not finish that final argument. The end of it smashed upon him in another way. The door came within his vision. As it swung inward he could not at first see whether it was open or closed. Leaning against the logs close to the door was a pair of long snowshoes and a bundle of javelins. A sickening disappointment swept over him as he stared at the javelins. A giant Eskimo and not a white man had made the trail they had followed. Their race against time had brought them straight to the rendezvous of their foes—and there would be no guns. In that moment when all the hopes he had built up seemed slipping away from under him he could see no other possible significance in the presence of the javelins. Then, for an instant, he held his breath and sniffed the air like a dog getting the wind. The cabin door was open. And out through that door came the mingling aroma of coffee and tobacco! An Eskimo might have tobacco, or even tea. But coffee—*never!*

Every drop of blood in his body pounded like tiny beating fists as he crossed silently and swiftly the short space between the corner of the cabin and the open door. For perhaps half a dozen seconds he closed his eyes to give his snow-strained vision an even chance with the man in the cabin. Then he looked in.

It was a small cabin. It was possibly not more than ten feet square inside, and at the far end of it was a fireplace from which rose the chimney through the roof. At first Philip saw nothing except the dim outlines of things. It was a moment or two before he made out the figure of a man stooping over the fire. He stepped over the threshold, making no sound. The occupant of the cabin straightened himself slowly, lifting with extreme care a pot of coffee from the embers. A glance at his broad back and his giant stature told Philip that he was not an Eskimo. He turned. Even then for an infinitesimal space he did not see Philip as he stood fronting the door with the light in his face. It was a white man's face—a face almost hidden in a thick growth of beard and a tangle of hair that fell to the shoulders. Another instant and he had seen the intruder and stood like one turned suddenly into stone.

Philip had leveled Celie's little revolver.

"I am Philip Raine of His Majesty's service, the Royal Mounted," he said. "Throw up your hands!"

The moment's tableau was one of rigid amazement on

one side, of waiting tenseness on the other. Philip believed that the shadow of his body concealed the size of the tiny revolver in his hand. Anyway it would be effective at that distance, and he expected to see the mysterious stranger's hands go over his head the moment he recovered from the shock that had apparently gone with the command. What did happen he expected least of all. The arm holding the pot of steaming coffee shot out and the boiling deluge hissed straight at Philip's face. He ducked to escape it, and fired. Before he could throw back the hammer of the little single-action weapon for a second shot the stranger was at him. The force of the attack sent them both crashing back against the wall of the cabin, and in the few moments that followed Philip blessed the providential forethought that had made him throw off his fur coat and strip for action. His antagonist was not an ordinary man. A growl like that of a beast rose in his throat as they went to the floor, and in that death-grip Philip thought of Bram.

More than once in watching the wolf-man he had planned how he would pit himself against the giant if it came to a fight, and how he would evade the close arm-to-arm grapple that would mean defeat for him. And this man was Bram's equal in size and strength. He realized with the swift judgment of the trained boxer that open fighting and the evasion of the other's crushing brute strength was his one hope. On his knees he flung himself backward, and struck out. The blow caught his antagonist squarely in the face before he had succeeded in getting a firm clinch, and as he bent backward under the force of the blow Philip exerted every ounce of his strength, broke the other's hold, and sprang to his feet.

He felt like uttering a shout of triumph. Never had the thrill of mastery and of confidence surged through him more hotly than it did now. On his feet in open fighting he had the agility of a cat. The stranger was scarcely on his feet before he was at him with a straight shoulder blow that landed on the giant's jaw with crushing force. It would have put an ordinary man down in a limp heap. The other's weight saved him. A second blow sent him reeling against the log wall like a sack of grain. And then in the half-gloom of the cabin Philip missed. He put all his effort in that third blow and as his clenched fist shot over the other's shoulder he was carried off his balance and found himself again in the clutch of his enemy's arms. This time a huge hand found his throat. The other he blocked with his left arm, while with his right he drove in short-arm jabs against neck and jaw. Their ineffectiveness amazed him. His guard-arm was broken upward, and to escape the certain result of two hands gripping at his throat he took a sudden foot-lock on his adversary, flung all his weight forward, and again they went to the floor of the cabin.

Neither caught a glimpse of the girl standing wide-eyed and terrified in the door. They rolled almost to her feet. Full in the light she saw the battered, bleeding face of the strange giant, and Philip's fist striking it again and again. Then she saw the giant's two hands, and why he was suffering that punishment. They were at Philip's throat—huge hairy hands stained with his own blood. A cry rose to her lips and the blue in her eyes darkened with the fighting fire of her ancestors. She darted across the room to the fire. In an instant she was back with a stick of wood in her hands. Philip saw her then—her streaming hair and white face above them, and the club fell. The hands at his throat relaxed. He swayed to his feet and with dazed eyes and a weird sort of laugh opened his arms. Celie ran into them. He felt her sobbing

and panting against him. Then, looking down, he saw that for the present the man who had made the strange snowshoe trail was as good as dead.

The air he was taking into his half strangled lungs cleared his head and he drew away from Celie to begin the search of the room. His eyes were more accustomed to the gloom, and suddenly he gave a cry of exultation. Against the end of the mud and stone fireplace stood a rifle and over the muzzle of this hung a belt and holster. In the holster was a revolver. In his excitement and joy his breath was almost a sob as he snatched it from the holster and broke it in the light of the door. It was a big Colt Forty-five—and loaded to the brim. He showed it to Celie, and thrust her to the door.

"Watch!" he cried, sweeping his arm to the open. "Just two minutes more. That's all I want—two minutes—and then—"

He was counting the cartridges in the belt as he fastened it about his waist. There were at least forty, two-thirds of them soft-nosed rifle. The caliber was .303 and the gun was a Savage. It was modern up to the minute, and as he threw down the lever enough to let him glimpse inside the breech he caught the glisten of cartridges ready for action. He wanted nothing more. The cabin might have held his weight in gold and he would not have turned toward it.

With the rifle in his hands he ran past Celie out into the day. For the moment the excitement pounding in his body had got beyond his power of control. His brain was running riot with the joyous knowledge of the might that lay in his hands now and he felt an overmastering desire to shout his triumph in the face of their enemies.

"Come on, you devils! Come on, come on," he cried. And then, powerless to restrain what was in him, he let out a yell.

From the door Celie was staring at him. A few moments before her face had been dead white. Now a blaze of color was surging back into her cheeks and lips and her eyes shone with the glory of one who was looking on more than triumph. From her own heart welled up a cry, a revelation of that wonderful thing throbbing in her breast which must have reached Philip's ears had there not in that same instant come another sound to startle them both into listening slience.

It was not far distant. And it was unmistakably an answer to Philip's challenge.

CHAPTER XXI

As they listened the cry came again. This time Philip caught in it a note that he had not detected before. It was not a challenge but the long-drawn *ma-too-ee* of an Eskimo who answers the inquiring hail of a comrade.

"He thinks it is the man in the cabin," exclaimed Philip, turning to survey the fringe of forest through which their trail had come. "If the others don't warn him there's going to be one less Eskimo on earth in less than three minutes!"

Another sound had drawn Celie back to the door. When she looked in the man she had stunned with the club was moving. Her call brought Philip, and placing her in the open door to keep watch he set swiftly to work to make sure of their prisoner. With the *babiche* thong he had taken from his enemies he bound him hand and foot. A shaft of light fell full on the giant's face and naked chest where it had been laid bare in the struggle and Philip was about to rise when a purplish patch of tattooing caught his eyes. He made out first the crude picture of a shark with huge gaping jaws struggling under the weight of a ship's anchor, and then, directly under this pigment colored *tatu*, the almost invisible letters of a name. He made them out one by one— B-l-a-k-e. Before the surname was the letter G.

"Blake," he repeated, rising to his feet. "*George* Blake—a sailor—and a white man!"

Blake, returning to consciousness, mumbled incoherently. In the same instant Celie cried out excitedly at the door.

"Oo-ee, Philip—Philip! *Se det! Se! Se!*" She drew back with a sudden movement and pointed out the door. Concealing himself as much as possible from outside observation Philip peered forth. Not more than a hundred and fifty yards away a dog team was approaching. There were eight dogs and instantly he recognized them as the small fox-faced Eskimo breed from the coast. They were dragging a heavily laden sledge and behind them came the driver, a furred and hooded figure squat of stature and with a voice that came now in the sharp clacking commands that Philip had heard in the company of Bram Johnson. From the floor came a groan, and for an instant Philip turned to find Blake's bloodshot eyes wide open and staring at him. The giant's bleeding lips were gathered in a snarl and he was straining at the *babiche* thongs that bound him. In that same moment Philip caught a glimpse of Celie. She, too, was staring—and at Blake. Her lips were parted, her eyes were big with amazement and as she looked she clutched her hands convulsively at her breast and uttered a low, strange cry. For the first time she saw Blake's face with the light full upon it. At the sound of her cry Blake's eyes went to her, and for the space of a second the imprisoned beast on the floor and the girl looking down on him made up a tableau that held Philip spellbound. Between them was recognition—an amazed and stonelike horror on the girl's part, a sudden and growing glare of bestial exultation in the eyes of the man.

Suddenly there came the Eskimo's voice and the yapping of dogs. It was the first Blake had heard. He swung his head toward the door with a great gasp and the *babiche* cut like whipcord under the strain of his muscles. Swift as a flash Philip thrust the muzzle of the big Colt against his prisoner's head.

"Make a sound and you're a dead man, Blake!" He warned. "We need that team, and if you so much as whisper during the next ten seconds I'll scatter your brains over the floor!"

They could hear the cold creak of the sledge-runners now, and a moment later the patter of many feet outside the door. In a single leap Philip was at the door. Another and he was outside, and an amazed Eskimo was looking into the round black eye of his revolver. It required no common language to make him understand what was required of him. He backed into the cabin with the revolver within two feet of his breast. Celie had caught up the rifle and was standing guard over Blake as though fearful that he might snap his bonds. Philip laughed joyously when he saw how quickly she understood that she was to level the rifle at the Kogmollock's breast and hold it there until he had made him a prisoner. She was wonderful. She was panting in her excitement. From the floor Blake had noticed that her little white finger was pressing gently against the trigger of the rifle. It had made him shudder. It made the Eskimo cringe a bit now as Philip tied his hands behind him. And Philip saw it, and his heart thumped. Celie was gloriously careless.

It was over inside of two minutes, and with an audible sigh of relief she lowered her rifle. Then she leaned it against the wall and ran to Blake. She was tremendously excited as she pointed down into the bloodstained face and tried to explain to Philip the reason for that strange and thrilling recognition he had seen between them. From her he looked at Blake. The look in the prisoner's face sent a cold shiver through him. There was no fear in it. It was filled with a deep and undisguised exultation. Then Blake looked at Philip, and laughed outright.

"Can't understand her, eh" he chuckled. "Well, neither can I. But I know what she's trying to tell you. Damned funny, ain't it?"

It was impossible for him to keep his eyes from shifting

to the door. There was expectancy in that glance. Then his glance shot almost fiercely at Philip.

"So you're Philip Raine, of the R. N. M. P., eh? Well, you've got me guessed out. My name is Blake, but the G don't stand for George, If you'll cut the cord off'n my legs so I can stand up or sit down I'll tell you something. I can't do very much damage with my hands hitched the way they are, and I can't talk layin' down cause of my Adam's apple chokin' me."

Philip seized the rifle and placed it again in Celie's hands, stationing her once more at the door.

"Watch—and listen," he said.

He cut the thongs that bound his prisoner's ankles and Blake struggled to his feet. When he fronted Philip the big Colt was covering his heart.

"Now—talk!" commanded Philip. "I'm going to give you half a minute to begin telling me what I want to know, Blake. You've brought the Eskimos down. There's no doubt of that. What do you want of this girl, and what have you done with her people?"

He had never looked into the eyes of a cooler man than Blake, whose blood-stained lips curled in a sneering smile even as he finished.

"I ain't built to be frightened," he said, taking his time about it. "I know your little games an' I've throwed a good many bluffs of my own in my time. You're lyin' when you say you'll shoot, an' you know your are. I may talk and I may not. Before I make up my mind I'm going to give you a bit of brotherly advice. Take that team out there and hit across the barren—*alone*. Understand? *Alone*. Leave the girl here. It's your one chance of missing what happened to—" He grinned and shrugged his huge shoulders.

"You mean Anderson—Olaf Anderson—and the others up at Bathurst Inlet?" questioned Philip chokingly.

Blake nodded.

Philip wondered if the other could hear the pounding of his heart. He had discovered in this moment what the department had been trying to learn for two years. It was this man—Blake—who was the mysterious white leader of the Kogmollocks, and responsible for the growing criminal record of the natives along Coronation Gulf. And he had just confessed himself the murderer of Olaf Anderson! His finger trembled for an instant against the trigger of his revolver. Then, staring into Blake's face, he slowly lowered the weapon until it hung at his side. Blake's eyes gleamed as he saw what he thought was his triumph.

"*It's* your one chance," he urged. "And there ain't no time to lose."

Philip had judged his man, and now he prayed for the precious minutes in which to play out his game. The Kogmollocks who had taken up their trail could not be far from the cabin now.

"Maybe you're right, Blake," he said hesitatingly. "I think, after her experience with Bram Johnson that she is about willing to return to her father. Where is he?"

Blake made no effort to disguise his eagerness. In the droop of Philip's shoulder, the laxness of the hand that held the revolver and the change in his voice Blake saw in his captor an apparent desire to get out of the mess he was in. A glimpse of Celie's frightened face turned for an instant from the door gave weight to his conviction. "He's down the Coppermine—about a hundred miles. So, Bram Johnson—"

His eyes were a sudden blaze of fire. "Took care of her

until your little rats waylaid him on the trail and murdered him," interrupted Philip. "See here, Blake. You be square with me and I'll be square with you. I haven't been able to understand a word of her lingo and I'm curious to know a thing or two before I go. Tell me who she is, and why you haven't killed her father, and what you're going to do with her and I won't waste another minute."

Blake leaned forward until Philip felt the heat of his breath.

"What do I *want* of her?" he demanded slowly. "Why, if you'd been five years without sight of a white woman, an' then you woke up one morning to meet an angel like *her* on the trail two thousand miles up in nowhere what would *you* want of her" I was stunned, plumb stunned, or I'd had her then. And after that, if it hadn't been for that devil with his wolves—"

"Bram ran away with her just as you were about to get her into your hands," supplied Philip, fighting to save time. "She didn't even know that you wanted her, Blake, so far as I can find out. It's all a mystery to her. I don't believe she's guessed the truth even now. How the devil did you do it" Playing the friend stunt, eh" And keeping yourself in the background while your Kogmollocks did the work? Was that it?"

Blake nodded. His face was darkening as he looked at Philip and the light in his eyes was changing to a deep and steady glare. In that moment Philip had failed to keep the exultation out of his voice. It shone on his face. And Blake saw it. A throaty sound rose out of his thick chest and his lips parted in a snarl as there surged through him a realization that he had been tricked.

In that interval Philip spoke.

"If I never sent up a real prayer to God before I'm sending it now, Blake," he said. "I'm thanking Him that you didn't have time to harm Celie Armin, an' I'm thanking Him that Bram Johnson had a soul in his body in spite of his warped brain and his misshapen carcass. And now I'm going to keep my word. I'm not going to lose another minute. Come!"

"You—you mean—"

"No, you haven't guessed it. We're not going over the Barren. We're going back to that cabin on the Coppermine, and you're going with us. And listen to this, Blake—listen hard! There may be fighting. If there is, I want you to sort of harden yourself to the fact that the first shot fired is going straight through your gizzard. Do I make myself clear? I'll shoot you deader than a slat mackerel the instant one of your little murderers show up on the trail. So tell this owl-faced heathen here to spread the glad tidings when his brothers come in—and spread it good. Quick about it! I'm not bluffing now."

CHAPTER XXII

IN Philip's eyes Blake saw his match now. And more. For three-quarters of a minute he talked swiftly to the Eskimo. Philip knew that he was giving the Kogmollock definite instructions as to the manner in which his rescue must be accomplished. But he knew also that Blake would emphasize the fact that it must not be in open attack, no matter how numerous his followers might be.

He hurried Blake through the door to the sledge and team. The sledge was heavily laden with the meat of a fresh caribou kill and from the quantity of flesh he dragged off into the snow Philip surmised that the cabin would very soon be the rendezvous of a small army of Eskimo. There was probably a thousand pounds of it. Retaining only a single quarter of this he made Celie comfortable and turned his attention to Blake. With *babiche* cord he resecured his prisoner with the "manacle-hitch," which gave him free play of one hand and arm—his left. Then he secured the Eskimo's whip and gave it to Blake.

"Now—drive!" He commanded. "Straight for the Coppermine, and by the shortest cut. This is as much your race as mine now, Blake. The moment I see a sign of anything wrong you're a dead man!"

"And you—are a fool!" gritted Blake. "Good God, what a fool!"

"Drive—and shut up!"

Blake snapped his whip and gave a short, angry command in Eskimo. The dogs sprang from their bellies to their feet and at another command were off over the trail. From the door of the cabin the Eskimo's little eyes shone with a watery eagerness as he watched them go. Celie caught a last glimpse of him as she looked back and her hands gripped more firmly the rifle which lay across her lap. Philip had given her the rifle and it had piled upon her a mighty responsibility. He had meant that she should use it if the emergency called for action, and that she was to especially watch Blake. Her eyes did not leave the outlaw's broad back as he ran on a dozen paces ahead of the dogs. She was ready for him if he tried to escape, and she would surely fire. Running close to her side Philip observed the tight grip of her hands on the weapon, and saw one little thumb pinched up against the safety ready for instant action. He laughed, and for a moment she looked up at him, flushing suddenly when she saw the adoration in his face.

"Blake's right—I'm a fool," he cried down at her in a low voice that thrilled with his worship of her. "I'm a fool for risking *you*, sweetheart. By going the other way I'd have you forever. They wouldn't follow far into the south, if at all. Mebby you don't realize what we're doing by hitting back to that father of yours. Do you?"

She smiled.

"And mebby when we get there we'll find him dead," he added. "Dead or alive, everything is up to Blake now and you must help me watch him."

He pantomimed this caution by pointing to Blake and the rifle. Then he dropped behind. Over the length of sledge and team he was thirty paces from Blake. At that distance he would drop him with a single shot from the Colt.

They were following the trail already made by the meat-laden sledge, and the direction was northwest. It was evident that Blake was heading at least in the right direction and Philip believed that it would be but a short time before they would strike the Coppermine. Once on the frozen surface of the big stream that flowed into the Arctic their immediate peril of an ambuscade would be over. Blake was surely aware of that. If he had in mind a plan for escaping it must of necessity take form before they reached the river

Where the forest thinned out and the edge of the Barren crept in Philip ran at Celie's side, but when the timber thickened and possible hiding places for their enemies appeared in the trail ahead he was always close to Blake, with the big Colt held openly in his hand. At these times Celie watched the back trail. From her vantage on the sledge her alert eyes took in every bush and thicket to the right and left of them, and when Philip was near or behind her she was looking at least a rifle-shot ahead of Blake. For three-quarters of an hour they had followed the single sledge trail when Blake suddenly gave a command that stopped the dogs. They had reached a crest which overlooked a narrow finger of the treeless Barren on the far side of which, possibly a third of a mile distant, was a dark fringe of spruce timber. Blake pointed toward this timber. Out of it was rising a dark column of resinous smoke.

"It's up to you," he said coolly to Philip. "Our trail crosses through that timber—and you see the smoke. I imagine there are about twenty of Upi's men there feeding on caribou. The herd was close beyond when they made the kill. Now if we go on they're most likely to see us, or their dogs get wind of us—and Upi is a blood thirsty old cutthroat. I don't want that bullet through my gizzard, so I'm tellin' you."

Far back in Blake's eyes there lurked a gleam which Philip did not like. Blake was not a man easily frightened, and yet he had given what appeared to be fair warning to his enemy. He came a step nearer, and said in a lower voice:

"Raine, that's just one of Upi's crowds. If you go on to the cabin we're heading for there'll be two hundred fighting men after you before the day is over, and they'll get you whether you kill me or not. You've still got the chance I gave you back there. Take it—if you ain't tired of life. Give me the girl—an' you hit out across the barren with the team."

"We're going on," replied Philip, meeting the other's gaze steadily. "You know your little murderers, Blake. If any one can get past them without being seen it's you. And you've got to do it. I'll kill you if you don't. The Eskimos may get us after that, but they won't harm her in your way. Understand? We're going the limit in this game. And I figure you're putting up the biggest stake. I've got a funny sort of feeling that you're going to cash in before we reach the cabin."

For barely an instant the mysterious gleam far back in Blake's eyes died out. There was the hard, low note in Philip's voice which carried conviction and Blake knew he was ready to play the hand which he held. With a grunt and a shrug of his shoulders he stirred up the dogs with a crack of his whip and struck out at their head due west. During the next half hour Philip's eyes and ears were ceaselessly on the alert. He traveled close to Blake, with the big Colt in his hand, watching every hummock and bit of cover as they came to it. He also watched Blake and in the end was convinced that in the back of the outlaw's head was a sinister scheme in which he had the utmost confidence in spite of his threats and the fact that they had successfully got around Upi's camp. Once or twice when their eyes happened to meet he caught in Blake's face a contemptuous coolness, almost a sneering exultation which the other could not quite conceal. It filled him with a scarcely definable uneasiness. He was positive that Blake realized he would carry out his threat at the least sign of treachery or the appearance of an enemy, and yet he could not free himself from the uncomfortable oppression that was beginning to take hold of him. He concealed it from Blake. He tried to fight it out of himself. Yet it persisted. It was something which seemed to hover in the air about him—the *feel* of danger which he could not see. And then Blake suddenly pointed ahead over an open plain and said:

"There is the Coppermine."

CHAPTER XXIII

A CRY from Celie turned his gaze from the broad white trail of ice that was the Coppermine, and as he looked she pointed eagerly toward a huge pinnacle of rock that rose like an oddly placed cenotaph out of the unbroken surface of the plain.

Blake grunted out a laugh in his beard and his eyes lit up with an unpleasant fire as they rested on her flushed face.

"She's tellin' you that Bram Johnson brought her this way," he chuckled. "Bram was a fool—like you!"

He seemed not to expect a reply from Philip, but urged the dogs down the slope into the plain. Fifteen minutes later they were on the surface of the river.

Philip drew a deep breath of relief, and he found that same relief in Celie's face when he dropped back to her side. As far as they could see ahead of them there was no forest. The Coppermine itself seemed to be swallowed up in the vast white emptiness of the Barren. There could be no surprise attack here, even at night. And yet there was something in Blake's face which kept alive within him the strange premonition of a near and unseen danger. Again and again he tried to shake off the feeling. He argued with himself against the unreasonableness of the thing that had begun to oppress him. Blake was in his power. It was impossible for him to escape, and the outlaw's life depended utterly upon his success in getting them safely to the cabin. It was not conceivable to suppose that Blake would sacrifice his life merely that they might fall into the hands of the Eskimos. And yet—

He watched Blake—watched him more and more closely as they buried themselves deeper in that unending chaos of the north. And Blake, it seemed to him, was conscious of that increasing watchfulness. He increased his speed. Now and then Philip heard a curious chuckling sound smothered in his beard, and after an hour's travel on the snow-covered ice of the river he could no longer dull his vision to the fact that the farther they progressed into the open country the more confident Blake was becoming. He did not question him. He realized the futility of attempting to force his prisoner into conversation. In that respect it was Blake who held the whip hand. He could lie or tell the truth, according to the humor of his desire. Blake must have guessed this thought in Philip's mind. They were traveling side by side when he suddenly laughed. There was an unmistakable irony in his voice when he said:

"It's funny, Raine, that I should like you, ain't it?" A man who's mauled you, an' threatened to kill you! I guess it's because I'm so cussed sorry for you. You're heading straight for the gates of hell, an' they're open—wide open."

"And you?"

This time Blake's laugh was harsher.

"I don't count—now," he said. "Since you've made up your mind not to trade me the girl for your life I've sort of dropped out of the game. I guess you're thinking I can hold Upi's tribe back. Well, I can't—not when you're getting this far up in their country. If we split the difference, and you gave me her, Upi would meet me half way. God, but you've spoiled a nice dream!"

"A dream?"

Blake uttered a command to the dogs.

"Yes—more'n that. I've got an igloo up there even finer than Upi's—all built of whalebone and ship's timbers. Think of *her* in that, Rain— with *me!* That's the dream you smashed!"

"And her father—and the others—"

This time there was a ferocious undercurrent in Blake's guttural laugh, as though Philip had by accident reminded him of something that both amused and enraged him.

"Don't you know how these Kogmollock heathen look on a father-in-law?" He asked. "He's sort of walkin' delegate over the whole bloomin' family. A god with two legs. The *others?* Why, we killed them. But Upi and his heathen wouldn't see anything happen to the old man when they found I was going to take the girl. That's why he's alive up there in the cabin now. Lord, what a mess you're heading into, Raine! And I'm wondering, after you kill me, and they kill you, *who'll have the girl?* There's a halfbreed in the tribe an' she'll probably go to him. The heathen themselves don't give a flip for women, you know. So it's certain to be the halfbreed."

He surged on ahead, cracking his whip, and crying out to the dogs. Philip believed that in those few moments he had spoken much that was truth. He had, without hesitation and of his own volition, confessed the murder of the companions of Celie's father, and he had explained in a reasonable way why Armin himself had been spared. These facts alone increased his apprehension. Unless Blake was utterly confident of the final outcome he would not so openly expose himself. He was even more on his guard after this.

For several hours after his brief fit of talking Blake made no effort to resume the conversation nor any desire to answer Philip when the latter spoke to him. A number of times it struck Philip that he was going the pace that would tire out both man and beast before night. He knew that in Blake's shaggy head there was a brain keenly and dangerously alive, and he noted the extreme effort he was making to cover distance with a satisfaction that was not unmixed of suspicion. By three o'clock in the afternoon they were thirty-five miles from the cabin in which Blake had become a prisoner. All that distance they had traveled through a treeless barren without a sign of life. It was between three and four when they began to strike timber once more, and Philip asked himself if it had been Blake's scheme to reach this timber before dusk. In places the spruce and banskian pine thickened until they formed dark walls of forest and whenever they approached these patches Philip commanded Blake to take the middle of the river. The width of the stream was a comforting protection. It was seldom less than two hundred yards from shore to shore and frequently twice that distance. From the possible ambuscades they passed only a rifle could be used effectively, and whenever there appeared to be the possibility of that danger Philip traveled close to Blake, with the revolver in his hand. The crack of a rifle even if the bullet should find its way home, meant Blake's life. Of that fact the outlaw could no longer have a doubt.

For an hour before the gray dusk of Arctic night began to gather about them Philip began to feel the effect of their strenuous pace. Hours of cramped inactivity on the sledge had brought into Celie's face lines of exhaustion. Since middle-afternoon the dogs had dragged at times in their traces. Now they were dead-tired. Blake, and Blake alone, seemed tireless. It was six o'clock when they entered a country that was mostly plain, with a thin fringe of timber along the shores. They had raced for nine hours, and had traveled fifty miles. It was here, in a wide reach of river, that Philip gave the command to halt.

His first caution was to secure Blake hand and foot, with his back resting against a frozen snow-hummock a dozen paces from the sledge. The outlaw accepted the situation with an indifference which seemed to Philip more forced than philosophical. After that, while Celie was walking back and forth to produce a warmer circulation in her numbed body, he hurried to the scrub timber that grew along the shore and returned with a small armful of dry wood. The fire he built was small, and concealed as much as possible by the sledge. Ten minutes sufficed to cook the meat for their supper. Then he stamped out the fire, fed the dogs, and made a comfortable nest of bear skins for himself and Celie, facing Blake. The night had thickened until he could make out only dimly the form of the outlaw against the snow-hummock. His revolver lay ready at his side. In that darkness he drew Celie close up into his arms. Her head lay on his breast. He buried his lips in the smothering sweetness of her hair, and her arms crept gently about his neck. Even then he did not take his eyes from Blake, nor for an instant did he cease to listen for other sounds than the deep breathing of the exhausted dogs. It was only a little while before the stars began to fill the sky. The gloom lifted slowly, and out of darkness rose the white world in a cold, shimmering glory. In that starlight he could see the glisten of Celie's hair as it covered them like a golden veil, and once or twice through the space that separated them he caught the flash of a strange fire in the outlaw's eyes. Both shores were visible. He could have seen the approach of a man two hundred yards away.

After a little he observed that Blake's head was drooping upon his chest, and that his breathing had become deeper. His prisoner, he believed, was asleep. And Celie, nestling on his chest, was soon in slumber. He alone was awake,—and watching. The dogs, flat on their bellies, were dead to the world. For an hour he kept his vigil. In that time he could not see that Blake moved. He heard nothing suspicious. And the night grew steadily brighter with the white glow of the stars. He held the revolver in his hand now. The starlight played on it in a steely glitter that could not fail to catch Blake's eyes should he awake.

And then Philip found himself fighting—fighting desperately to keep awake. Again and again his eyes closed, and he forced them open with an effort. He had planned that they would rest for two or three hours. The two hours were gone when for the twentieth time his eyes shot open, and he looked at Blake. The outlaw had not moved. His head hung still lower on his breast, and again—slowly— irresistibly—exhaustion closed Philip's eyes. Even then Philip was conscious of fighting against the overmastering desire to sleep. It seemed to him that he was struggling for hours, and all that time his subconsciousness was crying out for him to awake, struggling to rouse him to the nearness of a great danger. It succeeded at last. His eyes opened, and he stared in a dazed and half blinded way toward Blake. His first sensation was one of vast relief that he had awakened. The stars were brighter. The night was still. And there, a dozen paces from him was the snow-hummock.

But Blake—Blake—

His heart leapt into his throat.

Blake was gone!

CHAPTER XXIV

THE shock of the discovery that Blake had escaped brought Philip half to his knees before he thought of Celie. In an instant the girl was awake. His arm had tightened almost fiercely about her. She caught the gleam of his revolver, and in another moment she saw the empty space where their prisoner had been. Swiftly Philip's eyes traveled over the moonlit spaces about them. Blake had utterly disappeared. Then he saw the rifle, and breathed easier. For some reason the outlaw had not taken that, and it was a moment or two before the significance of the fact broke upon him. Blake must have escaped just as he was making that last tremendous fight to rouse himself. He had had no more than time to slink away into the shadows of the night, and had not paused to hazard a chance of securing the weapon that lay on the snow close to Celie. He had evidently believed that Philip was only half asleep, and in the moonlight he must have seen the gleam of the big revolver leveled over his captor's knee.

Leaving Celie huddled in her furs, Philip rose to his feet and slowly approached the snow hummock against which he had left his prisoner. The girl heard the startled exclamation that fell from his lips when he saw what had happened. Blake had not escaped alone. Running straight out from behind the hummock was a furrow in the snow like the trail made by an otter. He had seen such furrows before, where Eskimos had wormed their way foot by foot within striking distance of dozing seals. Assistance had come to Blake in that manner, and he could see where—on their hands and knees—two men instead of one had stolen back through the moonlight.

Celie came to his side now, gripping the rifle in her hands.

Her eyes were wide and filled with frightened inquiry as she looked from the telltale trails in the snow into Philip's face. He was glad that she could not question him in words. He slipped the Colt into its holster and took the rifle from her hands. In the emergency which he anticipated the rifle would be more effective. That something would happen very soon he was positive. If one Eskimo had succeeded in getting ahead of his comrades to Blake's relief others of Upi's tribe must be close behind. And yet he wondered, as he thought of this, why Blake and the Kogmollock had not killed him instead of running away. The truth he told frankly to Celie, thankful that she could not understand.

"It was the gun," he said. "They thought I had only closed my eyes, and wasn't asleep. If something hadn't kept that gun leveled over my knee—" He tried to smile, knowing that with every second the end might come for them from out of the gray mist of moonlight and shadow that shrouded the shore. "It was a one-man job, sneaking out like that, and there's sure a bunch of them coming up fast to take a hand in the game. It's up to us to hit the high spots, my dear—and you might pray God to give us time for a start."

If he had hoped to keep from her the full horror of their situation, he knew, as he placed her on the sledge, that he had failed. Her eyes told him that. Intuitively she had guessed at the heart of the thing, and suddenly her arms reached up about his neck as he bent over her and against his breast he heard the sobbing cry that she was trying hard to choke back. Under the cloud of her hair her warm, parted lips lay for a thrilling moment against his own, and then he sprang to the dogs. They had already roused themselves and at his command began sullenly to drag their lame and exhausted bodies into trace formation. As the sledge began to move he sent the long lash of the driving whip curling viciously over the backs of the pack and the pace increased. Straight ahead of them ran the white trail of the Coppermine, and they were soon following this with the eagerness of a team on the homeward stretch. As Philip ran behind he made a fumbling inventory of the loose rifle cartridges in the pocket of his coat, and under his breath prayed to God that the day would come before the Eskimos closed in. Only one thing did he see ahead of him now—a last tremendous fight for Celie, and he wanted the light of dawn to give him accuracy. He had thirty cartridges, and it was possible that he could put up a successful running fight until they reached Armin's cabin. After that fate would decide. He was already hatching a scheme in his brain. If he failed to get Blake early in the fight which he anticipated he would show the white flag, demand a parley with the outlaw under pretense of surrendering Celie, and shoot him dead the moment they stood face to face. With Blake out of the way there might be another way of dealing with Upi and his Kogmollocks. It was Blake who wanted Celie. In Upi's eyes there were other things more precious than a woman. The thought revived in him a new thrill of hope. It recalled to him the incident of Father Breault and the white woman nurse who, farther west, had been held for ransom by the Nanamalutes three years ago. Not a hair of the woman's head had been harmed in nine months of captivity. Olaf Anderson had told him the whole story. There had been no white man there— only the Eskimos, and with the Eskimos he believed that he could deal now if he succeeded in killing Blake. Back at the cabin he could easily have settled the matter, and he felt like cursing himself for his shortsightedness.

In spite of the fact that he had missed his main chance

he began now to see more than hope in a situation that five minutes before had been one of appalling gloom. If he could keep ahead of his enemies until daybreak he had a ninety percent chance of getting Blake. At some spot where he could keep the Kogmollock's at bay and scatter death among them if they attacked he would barricade himself and Celie behind the sledge and call out his acceptance of Blake's proposition to give up Celie as the price of his own safety. He would demand an interview with Blake, and it was then that his opportunity would come.

But ahead of him were the leaden hours of the gray night! Out of that ghostly mist of pale moonlight through which the dogs were traveling like sinuous shadows Upi and his tribe could close in on him silently and swiftly, unseen until they were within striking distance. In that event all would be lost. He urged the dogs on, calling them by the name which he had heard Blake use, and occasionally he sent the long lash of his whip curling over their backs. The surface of the Coppermine was smooth and hard. Now and then they came to stretches of glare ice and at these intervals Philip rode behind Celie, staring back into the white mystery of the night out of which they had come. It was so still that the *click, click, click* of the dogs' claws sounded like the swift beat of tiny castanets on the ice. He could hear the panting breath of the beasts. The whalebone runners of the sledge creaked with the shrill protest of steel traveling over frozen snow. Beyond these sounds there were no others, with the exception of his own breath and the beating of his own heart. Mile after mile of the Coppermine dropped behind them. The last tree and the last fringe of bushes disappeared, and to the east, the north, and the west there was no break in the vast emptiness of the great Arctic plain. Ever afterward the memory of that night seemed like a grotesque and horrible dream to him. Looking back, he could remember how the moon sank out of the sky and utter darkness closed them in and how through that darkness he urged on the tired dogs, tugging with them at the lead-trace, and stopping now and then in his own exhaustion to put his arms about Celie and repeat over and over again that everything was all right. After an eternity the dawn came. What there was to be of day followed swiftly, like the Arctic night. The shadows faded away, the shores loomed up and the illimitable sweep of the plain lifted itself into vision as if from out of a great sea of receding fog. In the quarter hour's phenomenon between the last of darkness and wide day Philip stood straining his eyes southward over the white path of the Coppermine. It was Celie, huddled close at his side, who turned her eyes first from the trail their enemies would follow. She faced the north, and the cry that came from her lips brought Philip about like a shot. His first sensation was one of amazement that they had not yet passed beyond the last line of timber. Not more than a third of a mile distant the river ran into a dark strip of forest that reached in from the western plain like a great finger. Then he saw what Celie had seen. Close up against the timber a spiral of smoke was rising into the air. He made out in another moment the form of a cabin, and the look in Celie's staring face told him the rest. She was sobbing breathless words which he could not understand, but he knew that they had won their race, and that it was Armin's place. And Armin was not dead. He was alive, as Blake had said—and it was about breakfast time. He had held up under the tremendous strain of the night until now— and now he was filled with an uncontrollable desire to laugh. The curious thing about it was that in spite of this desire no sound came from his throat. He continued to stare until Celie turned to him and swayed into his arms. In the moment of their triumph her strength was utterly gone. And then the thing happened which brought the life back into him again with a shock. From far up the black finger of timber where it bellied over the horizon of the plain there floated down to them a chorus of sound. It was a human sound— the yapping, wolfish cry of an Eskimo horde closing in on man or beast. They had heard that same cry close on the heels of the fight in the clearing. Now it was made by many voices instead of two or three. It was accompanied almost instantly by the clear, sharp report of a rifle, and a moment later the single shot was followed by a scattering fusillade. After that there was silence.

Quickly Philip bundled Celie on the sledge and drove the dogs ahead, his eyes on a wide opening in the timber three or four hundred yards above the river. Five minutes later the sledge drew up in front of the cabin. In that time they heard no further outcry or sound of gunfire, and from the cabin itself there came no sign of life, unless the smoke meant life. Scarcely had the sledge stopped before Celie was on her feet and running to the door. It was locked, and she beat against it excitedly with her little fists, calling a strange name. Standing close behind her, Philip heard a shuffling movement beyond the log walls, the scraping of a bar, and a man's voice so deep that it had in it the booming note of a drum. To it Celie replied with almost a shriek. The door swung inward, and Philip saw a man's arms open and Celie run into them. He was an old man. His hair and beard were white. This much Philip observed before he turned with a sudden thrill toward the open in the forest. Only he had heard the cry that had come from that direction, and now, looking back, he saw a figure running swiftly over the plain toward the cabin. Instantly he knew that it was a white man. With his revolver in his hand he advanced to meet him and in a brief space they stood face to face.

The stranger was a giant of a man. His long, reddish hair fell to his shoulders. He was bareheaded, and panting as if hard run, and his face was streaming with blood. His eyes seemed to bulge out of their sockets as he stared at Philip. And Philip, almost dropping his revolver in his amazement, gasped incredulously:

"My God, is it you—Olaf Anderson!"

CHAPTER XXV

FOLLOWING that first wild stare of uncertainty and disbelief in the big Swede's eyes came a look of sudden and joyous recognition. He was clutching at Philip's hand like a drowning man before he made an effort to speak, still with his eyes on the other's face as if he was not quite sure they had not betrayed him. Then he grinned. There was only one man in the world who could grin like Olaf Anderson. In spite of blood and swollen features it transformed him. Men loved the red-headed Swede because of that grin. Not a man in the service who knew him but swore that Olaf would die with the grin on his face, because the tighter the hole he was in the more surely would the grin be there. It was the grin that answered Philip's question.

"Just in time—to the dot," said Olaf, still pumping Philip's hand, and grinning hard. "All dead but me—Calkins, Harris, and that little Dutchman, O'Flynn. Cold and stiff, Phil, every one of them. I knew an investigating patrol would be coming up pretty soon. Been looking for it every day. How many men you got?"

He looked beyond Philip to the cabin and the sledge. The grin slowly went out of his face, and Philip heard the sudden catch in his breath. A swift glance revealed the amazing truth to Olaf. He dropped Philip's hand and stepped back, taking him in suddenly from head to foot.

"Alone?"

"Yes, alone," nodded Philip. "With the exception of Celie Armin. I brought her back to her father. A fellow named Blake is back there a little way with Upi's tribe. We beat them out, but I'm figuring it won't be long before they show up."

The grin was fixed in Olaf's face again.

"Lord bless us, but it's funny," he grunted. "They're coming on the next train, so to speak, and right over in that neck of woods is the other half of Upi's tribe chasing their short legs off to get me. And the comical part of it is you're *alone!*" His eyes were fixed suddenly on the revolver. "Ammunition?" he demanded eagerly. "And—grub?"

"Thirty or forty rounds of rifle, a dozen Colt, and plenty of meat—"

"Then into the cabin, and the dogs with us," almost shouted the Swede.

From the edge of the forest came the report of a rifle and over their heads went the humming drone of a bullet.

They were back at the cabin in a dozen seconds, tugging at the dogs. It cost an effort to get them through the door, with the sledge after them. Half a dozen shots came from the forest. A bullet spattered against the log wall, found a crevice, and something metallic jingled inside. As Olaf swung the door shut and dropped the wooden bar in place Philip turned for a moment toward Celie. She went to him, her eyes shining in the semi-gloom of the cabin, and put her arms up about his shoulders. The Swede, looking on, stood transfixed, and the white-bearded Armin stared incredulously. On her tip-toes Celie kissed Philip, and then turning with her arms still about him said something to the older man that brought an audible gasp from Olaf. In another moment she had slipped away from Philip and back to her father. The Swede was flattening his face against a two inch crevice between the logs when Philip went to his side.

"What did she say, Olaf?" he entreated.

"That she's going to marry you if we ever get out of this hell of a fix we're in," grunted Olaf. "Pretty lucky dog, I say, if it's true. Imagine Celie Armin marrying a dub like you! But it will never happen. If you don't believe it fill your eyes with that out there!"

Philip glued his eyes to the long crevice between the logs and found the forest and the little finger of plain between straight in his vision. The edge of the timber was alive with men. There must have been half a hundred of them and they were making no effort to conceal themselves. For the first time Olaf began to give him an understanding of the situation.

"This is the fortieth day we've held them off," he said, in the quick-cut, business-like voice he might have used in rendering a report to a superior. "Eighty cartridges to begin with and a month's ration of grub for two. All but the three last cartridges went day before yesterday. Yesterday everything quiet. On the edge of starvation this morning when I went out on scout duty and to take a chance at game. Surprised a couple of them carrying meat and had a tall fight. Others hove into action and I had to use two of my cartridges. One left—and they're showing themselves because they know we don't dare to use ammunition at long range. My caliber is thirty-five. What's yours?"

"The same," replied Philip quickly, his blood beginning to thrill with the anticipation of battle. "I'll give you half. I'm on duty from Fort Churchill, off on a tangent of my own." He did not take his eyes from the slit in the wall as he told Anderson in a hundred words what had happened since his meeting with Bram Johnson. "And with forty cartridges we'll give 'em a taste of hell," he added.

He caught his breath, and the last word half choked itself from his lips. He knew that Anderson was staring as hard as he. Up from the river and over the level sweep of plain between it and the timber came a sledge, followed by a second, a third, and a fourth. In the trail behind the sledges trotted a score and a half of fur-clad figures.

"It's Blake!" exclaimed Philip.

Anderson drew himself away from the wall. In his eyes burned a curious greenish flame, and his face was set with the hardness of iron. In that iron was molded indistinctly the terrible smile with which he always went into battle or fronted "his man." Slowly he turned, pointing a long arm at each of the four walls of the cabin.

"That's the lay of the fight," he said, making his words short and to the point. "They can come at us on all sides, and so I've made a six-foot gun-crevice in each wall. We can't count on Armin for anything but the use of a club if it comes to close quarters. The walls are built of saplings and they've got guns out there that get through. Outside of that we've got one big advantage. The little devils are superstitious about fighting at night, and even Blake can't force them into it. Blake is the man I was after when I ran across Armin and his people. *Gad!*"

There was an unpleasant snap in his voice as he peered through the gun-hole again. Philip looked across the room to Celie and her father as he divided the cartridges. They were both listening, yet he knew they did not understand what he and Olaf were saying. He dropped a half of the cartridges into the right hand pocket of the Swede's service coat, and advanced then toward Armin with both his hands held out in greeting. Even in that tense moment he saw the sudden flash of pleasure in Celie's eyes. Her lips trembled, and she spoke softly and swiftly to her father, looking at Philip. Armin advanced a step, and their hands met. At first Philip had taken him for an old man. Hair and beard were white, his shoulders were bent, his hands were long and thin. But his eyes, sunken deep in their sockets, had not aged with the rest of him. They were filled with the piercing scrutiny of a hawk's as they looked into his own, measuring him in that moment so far as man can measure man. Then he spoke, and it was the light in Celie's eyes, her parted lips, and the flush that came swiftly into her face that gave him an understanding of what Armin was saying.

From the end of the cabin Olaf's voice broke in. With it came the metallic working of his rifle as he filled the chamber with cartridges. He spoke first to Celie and Armin in their own language, then to Philip.

"It's a pretty safe gamble we'd better get ready for them," he said. "They'll soon begin. Did you split even on the cartridges?"

"Seventeen apiece."

"Philip examined his rifle, and looked through the gun-crevice toward the forest. He heard Olaf tugging at the dogs as he tied them to the bunk posts; he heard Armin say something in a strained voice, and the Swede's unintelligible reply, followed by a quick, low-voiced interrogation from Celie. In the same moment his heart gave a sudden jump. In the fringe of the forest he saw a long, thin line of moving figures—advancing. He did not call out a warning instantly. For a space in which he might have taken a long breath or two his eyes and brain were centered on the moving figures and the significance of their drawn-out formation. Like a camera-flash his eyes ran over the battleground. Half way between the cabin and that fringe of forest four hundred yards away was a "hogback" in the snow, running a curving parallel with the plain. It formed scarcely more than a three or four foot rise in the surface, and he had given it no special significance until now. His lips formed words as the thrill of understanding leapt upon him.

"They're moving!" He called to Olaf.

"They're going to make a rush for the little ridge between us and the timber. Good God, Anderson, there's an army of them!"

"Not more'n a hundred," replied the Swede calmly, taking his place at the gun-crevice. "Take it easy, Phil This will be good target practice. We've got to make an eighty percent kill as they come across the open. This is mighty comfortable compared with the trick they turned on us when they got Calkins, Harris and O'Flynn. I got away in the night."

The moving line had paused just within the last straggling growth of trees, as if inviting the fire of the defenders.

Olaf grunted as he looked along the barrel of his rifle.

"Strategy," he mumbled. "They know we're shy of ammunition."

In the moments of tense waiting Philip found his first opportunity to question the man at his side. First, he said:

"I guess mebby you understand, Olaf. We've gone through a hell together, and I love her. If we get out of this she's going to be my wife. She's promised me that, and yet I swear to Heaven I don't know more than a dozen words of her language. What has happened? Who is she? Why was she with Bram Johnson? You know their language, and have been with them—?

"They're taking final orders," interrupted Olaf, as if he had not heard. "There's something more on foot than a rush to the ridge. It's Blakes's scheming. See those little groups forming? They're going to bring battering-rams, and make a second rush from the ridge." He drew in a deep breath, and without a change in the even tone of his voice, went on:

"Calkins, Harris and O'Flynn went down in a good fight. Tell you about that later. Hit seven days' west, and run on the camp of Armin, his girl, and two white men—Russians— guided by two Kogmollocks from Coronation Gulf. You can guess some of the rest. The little devils had Blake and his gang about us two days after I struck them. Bram Johnson and his wolves came along then—from nowhere—going nowhere. The Kogmollocks think Bram is a great Devil, and that each of his wolves is a Devil. If it hadn't been for that they would have murdered us in a hurry, and Blake would have taken the girl. They were queered by the way Bram would squat on his haunches, and stare at her. The second day I saw him mumbling over something, and looked sharp. He had one of Celie's long hairs, and when he saw me he snarled like an animal, as though he feared I would take it from him. I knew what was coming. I knew Blake was only waiting for Bram to get away from his Kogmollocks—so I told Celie to give Bram a strand of her hair. She did—with her own hands, and from that minute the madman watched her like a dog. I tried to talk with him, but couldn't. I didn't seem to be able to make him understand. And then—"

The Swede cut himself short.

"They're moving, Phil! Take the men with the battering rams—and let them get half way before you fire!. . .You see, Bram and his wolves had to have meat. Blake attacked while he was gone. Russians killed—Armin and I cornered, fighting for the girl behind us, when Bram came back like a burst of thunder. He didn't fight. He grabbed the girl, and was off with her like the wind with his wolf-team. Armin and I got into this cabin, and have been here—forty days and nights—"

His voice stopped ominously. A fraction of a second later

it was followed by the roar of his rifle, and at the first shot
one of Blake's Kogmollocks crumpled up with a grunt half
way between the snowridge and the forest.

CHAPTER XXVI

THE Eskimos were advancing at a trot now over the open space. Philip was amazed at their number. There were at least a hundred, and his heart choked with a feeling of despair even as he pulled the trigger for his first shot. He had seen the effect of Olaf's shot, and following the Swede's instructions aimed for his man in the nearest group behind the main line. He did not instantly see the result, as a puff of smoke shut out his vision, but a moment later, aiming again, he saw a dark blotch left in the snow. From his end of the crevice Olaf had seen the man go down, and he grunted his approbation. There were five of the groups bearing tree trunks for battering-rams, and on one of these Philip concentrated the six shots in his rifle. Four of the tree-bearers went down, and the two that were left dropped their burden and joined those ahead of them. Until Philip stepped back to reload his gun he had not noticed Celie. She was close at his side, peering through the gun-hole at the tragedy out on the plain. Once before he had been astounded by the look in her face when they had been confronted by great danger, and as his fingers worked swiftly in refilling the magazine of his rifle he saw it there again. It was not fear, even now. It was a more wonderful thing than that. Her wide-open eyes glowed with a strange, dark luster; in the center of each of her cheeks was a vivid spot of color, and her lips were parted slightly, so that he caught the faintest gleam of her teeth. Wonderful as a fragile flower she stood there with her eyes upon him, her splendid courage and her faith in him flaming within her like a fire

And then he heard Anderson's voice

"They're behind the ridge. We got eight of them."

In half a dozen places Philip had seen where bullets had bored the way through the cabin, and leaning his gun against the wall, he sprang to Celie and almost carried her behind the bunk that was built against the logs.

"You must stay here," he cried. "Do you understand? *Here!*"

She nodded, and smiled. It was a wonderful smile—a flash of tenderness telling him that she knew what he was saying, and that she would obey him. She made no effort to detain him with her hands, but in that moment—if life had been the forfeit—Philip would have stolen the precious time in which to take her in his arms. For a space he held her close to him, his lips crushed to hers, and faced the wall again with the throb of her soft breast still beating against his heart. He noticed Armin standing near the door, his hand resting on a huge club which, in turn, rested on the floor. Calmly he was waiting for the final rush. Olaf was peering through the gun-hole again. And then came what he had expected—a rattle of fire from the snow-ridge. The *pit—pit—pit* of bullets rained against the cabin in a dull tattoo. Through the door came a bullet, sending a splinter close to Armin's face. Almost in the same instant a second followed it, and a third came through the crevice so close to Philip that he felt the hissing breath of it in his face. One of the dogs emitted a wailing howl and flopped among its comrades in uncanny convulsions.

Olaf staggered back, and faced Philip. There was no trace of the fighting grin in his face now. It was set like an iron mask.

"*Get down!*" he shouted. "Do you hear, *get down!*" He dropped on his knees, crying out the warning to Armin in the other's language. "They've got enough guns to make a sieve of this kennel if their ammunition holds out—and the lower logs are the heaviest. Flatten yourself out until they stop firing, with your feet toward 'em, like this," and he stretched himself out on the floor, parallel with the direction of fire.

In place of following the Swede's example Philip ran to Celie. Half way a bullet almost got him, flipping the collar of his shirt. He dropped beside her and gathered her up completely in his arms, with his own body between her and the fire. A moment later he thanked God for the protection of the bunk. He heard the ripping of a bullet through the saplings and caught distinctly the thud of it as the spent lead dropped to the floor. Celie's head was close on his breast, her eyes were on his face, her soft lips so near he could feel their breath. He kissed her, unbelieving even then that the end was near for her. It was monstrous—impossible. Lead was finding its way into the cabin like raindrops. He heard the Swede's voice again, crying thickly from the floor:

"Hug below the lower log. You've got eight inches. If you rise above that they'll get you." He repeated the warning to Armin.

As if to emphasize his words there came a howl of agony from another of the dogs.

Still closer Philip held the girl to him. Her hands had crept convulsively to his neck. He crushed his face down against hers, and waited. It came to him suddenly that Blake must be reckoning on this very protection which he was giving Celie. He was gambling on the chance that while the male defenders of the cabin would be wounded or killed Celie would be sheltered until the last moment from their fire. If that was so, the firing would soon cease until Blake learned results.

Scarcely had he made this guess when the fusillade ended.

Instead of rifle-fire there came a sudden strange howl of voices and Olaf sprang to his feet. Philip had risen, when the Swede's voice came to him in a choking cry. Prepared for the rush he had expected, Olaf was making an observation through the gun-crevice. Suddenly, without turning his head, he yelled back at them:

"Good God—it's Bram—*Bram Johnson!*"

Even Celie realized the thrilling import of the Swede's excited words. *Bram Johnson!* She was only a step behind Philip when he reached the wall. With him she looked out. Out of that finger of forest they were coming—Bram and his wolves! The pack was free, spreading out fan-shape, coming like the wind! Behind them was Bram—a wild and monstrous figure against the whiteness of the plain, bearing in his hand a giant club. His yell came to them. It rose above all other sound, like the cry of a great beast. The wolves came faster, and then—

The truth fell upon those in the cabin with a suddenness that stopped the beating of their hearts.

Bram Johnson and his wolves were attacking the Eskimos!

From the thrilling spectacle of the giant madman charging over the plain behind his ravenous beasts Philip shifted his amazed gaze to the Eskimos. They were no longer concealing themselves. Palsied by a strange terror, they were staring at the onrushing horde and the shrieking wolf-man. In those first appalling moments of horror and stupefaction not a gun was raised or a shot fired. Then there rose from the ranks of the Kogmollocks a strange and terrible cry, and in another moment the plain between the forest and the snow-ridge was alive with fleeing creatures in whose heavy brains surged the monstrous thought that they were attacked not by man and beast, but by devils. And in that same moment it seemed that Bram Johnson and his wolves were among them. From man to man the beasts leapt, driven on by the shrieking voice of their master; and now Philip saw the giant madman overtake one after another of the running figures, and saw the crushing force of his club as it fell. Celie swayed back from the wall and stood with her hands to her face. The Swede sprang past her, flung back the bar to the door, and opened it. Philip was a step behind him. From the front of the cabin they began firing, and man after man crumpled down under their shots. If Bram and his wolves sensed the shooting in the ferocity of their blood-lust they paid no more attention to it than to the cries for mercy that rose chokingly out of the throats of their enemies. In another sixty seconds the visible part of it was over. The last of the Kogmollocks disappeared into the edge of the forest. After them went the wolf-man and his pack.

Philip faced his companion. His gun was hot—and empty. The old grin was in Olaf's face. In spite of it he shuddered.

"We won't follow," he said. "Bram and his wolves will attend to the trimmings, and he'll come back when the job is finished. Meanwhile, we'll get a little start for home, eh? I'm tired of this cabin. Forty days and nights—*ugh!* It was *hell.* Have you a spare pipeful of tobacco, Phil? If you have— let's see, where did I leave off in that story about Princess Celie and the Duke of Rugni?"

"The—the—*what?*"

"Your tobacco, Phil!"

In a dazed fashion Philip handed his tobacco pouch to the Swede.

"You said—Princess Celie—The Duke of Rugni—"

Olaf nodded as he stuffed his pipe bowl.

"That's it. Armin is the Duke of Rugni, whatever Rugni

is. He was chased off to Siberia a good many years ago, when Celie was a kid, that somebody else could get hold of the Dukedom. Understand? Millions in it, I suppose. He says some of Rasputin's old friends were behind it, and that for a long time he was kept in the dungeons of the fortress of St. Peter and St. Paul, with the Neva River running over his head. The friends he had, most of them in exile or chased out of the country, thought he was dead, and some of these friends were caring for Celie. Just after Rasputin was killed, and before the Revolution broke out, they learned Armin was alive and dying by inches somewhere up on the Siberian coast. Celie's mother was Danish—died almost before Celie could remember; but some of her relatives and a bunch of Russian exiles in London framed up a scheme to get Armin back, chartered a ship, sailed with Celie on board, and—"

Olaf paused to light his pipe.

"And they found the Duke," he added. "They escaped with him before they learned of the Revolution, or Armin could have gone home with the rest of the Siberian exiles and claimed his rights. For a lot of reasons they put him aboard an American whaler, and the whaler missed its plans by getting stuck in the ice for the winter up in Coronation Gulf. After that they started out with dogs and sledge and guides. There's a lot more, but that's the meat of it, Phil. I'm going to leave it to you to learn Celie's language and get the details first-hand from her. But she's a right enough princess, old man. And her dad's a duke. It's up to you to Americanize 'em. Eh, what's that?"

Celie had come from the cabin and was standing at Philip's side, looking up into his face, and the light which Olaf saw unhidden in her eyes make him laugh softly:

"And you've got the job half done, Phil. The Duke may go

back and raise the devil with the people who put him in cold storage, but Lady Celie is going to like America. Yessir, she's going to like it better'n any other place on the face of the earth!"

. . . .

It was late that afternoon, traveling slowly southward over the trail of the Coppermine, when they heard far behind them the wailing cry of Bram Johnson's wolves. The sound came only once, like the swelling surge of a sudden sweep of wind, yet when they camped at the beginning of darkness Philip was confident the madman and his pack were close behind them. Utter exhaustion blotted out the hours for Celie and himself, while Olaf, buried in two heavy Eskimo coats he had foraged from the field of battle, sat on guard through the night. Twice in the stillness of his long vigil he heard strange cries. Once it was the cry of a beast. The second time it was that of a man.

The second day, with dogs, refreshed, they traveled faster, and it was this night that they camped in the edge of timber and built a huge fire. It was such a fire as illumined the space about them for fifty paces or more, and it was into this light that Bram Johnson stalked, so suddenly and so noiselessly that a sharp little cry sprang from Celie's lips, and Olaf and Philip and the Duke of Rugni stared in wide-eyed amazement. In his right hand the wolf-man bore a strange object. It was an Eskimo coat, tied into the form of a bag, and in the bottom of this improvision was a lump half the size of a water pail. Bram seemed oblivious of all presence but that of Celie. His eyes were on her alone as he advanced and with a weird sound in his throat deposited the bundle at her feet. In another moment he was gone. The Swede rose slowly from where he was sitting, and speaking casually to Celie, took the wolf-man's gift up in his hands. Philip observed the strange look in his face as he turned his back to Celie in the firelight and opened the bag sufficiently to get a look inside. Then he walked out in to the darkness, and a moment later returned without the bundle, and with a laugh apologized to Celie for his action.

"No need of telling her what it was," he said to Philip then. "I explained that it was foul meat Bram had brought in as a present. As a matter of fact it was Blake's head. You know the Kogmollocks have a pretty habit of pleasing a friend by presenting him with the head of a dead enemy. Nice little package for her to have opened, eh?"

. . . .

After all, there are some very strange happenings in life, and the adventurers of the Royal Northwest Mounted Police come upon their share. The case of Bram Johnson, the mad wolf-man of the Upper Country, happened to be one of them, and filed away in the archives of the Department is a big envelope filled with official and personal documents, signed and sworn to by various people. There is, for instance, the brief and straightforward deposition of Corporal Olaf Anderson, of the Fort Churchill Division, and there is the longer and more detailed testimony of Mr. and Mrs. Philip Raine and the Duke of Rugni; and attached to these depositions is a copy of an official decision pardoning Bram Johnson and making of him a ward of the great Dominion instead of a criminal. He is no longer hunted. "Let Bram Johnson alone" is the word that had gone forth to the man-

David M. Hartford's Production.
LEWIS STONE, WALLACE BEERY AND RUTH RENICK IN THE PHOTOPLAY.
A First National Attraction.

hunters of the Service. It is a wise and human judgment. Bram's country is big and wild. And he and his wolves still hunt there under the light of the moon and the stars.

THE END